MINATO SKETCHES

Minato Sketches

a novel

by

Sharon White

MINERVA RISING PRESS

Glen Ellyn

ISBN 978-1-950811-23-6

Cover image by Harrison Lin

First Printing January 2025

Published by Minerva Rising Press
864 Western Avenue
Glen Ellyn, IL 60137
www.minervarising.com

For Graham

MAY

Ebb Tide Harbor

ONE

As she came down out of the clouds, Gigi saw shiny fields, wet with a sheen of green water and the spiky hills she remembered. The villages were tucked into crevices between the islands of trees and rocks and fields. She'd read about how all the paper houses had burned long ago. But there were certainly paper houses hidden along the shining river. And more folded in the curves and lumps of the hills.

Near the city, long white egrets appeared. Silent, floating on the wind. Squat cormorants raced down the dark rivers. Everything was different. The last few years replaced with concrete that somehow seemed more alive than she remembered. Bending and curving above the canals.

So the woman who told her about the fires in the city during the Pacific War was right. Most of the paper houses had vanished in Tokyo. In the morning she watched as armies of salary workers marched to offices, their faces placid with sleep. One eyebrow raised here, another foot placed there. Such precision and pizazz. Every now and then someone would break rank and get a coffee at one of the cafés. Folding and unfolding a paper. Picking a white cup off a table and then putting it down.

That night she ended up on a street with noodle stalls. Large blue fish slept in tanks arrayed along the walls. She could see them breathing in the dusk of their containers. Men in white shirts and black pants jostled against each other, banging their briefcases on their thighs. Everything was lit with a burning core.

These men had been at work forever. Toting their bags from home to trains to the office to the narrow streets where food was displayed on plastic cards or in bowls with plastic wrap. Old women beckoned customers in at the doors. Cloth banners with beautiful letters hung from every open window.

So many drunk men rubbing their bellies, dancing in knots close to each other, just about to fight. *No English Here*, one sign said. Inside the stall it was quiet. A cook cocked his head and looked away. It was cool, so cool she pulled her sweater closer. She'd left two grown boys and a husband in a country far away.

Everything was alive around her.

TWO

Her new boss said, "I'm part Celtic and part Quebecois. I have friends all over the place. I've been important in more universities than you can count. I'm a denizen of this place, a wow guy. Why do you think I got this job in Tokyo?"

He sat at his large desk, pictures of important looking people arranged on the shelves behind him. He had on a short-sleeved shirt and his arms were very tan.

"Have you had a stroke?" He asked and leaned forward. "I know I may have seen that in your documents. Are you sure you haven't had a stroke?"

She adjusted her smile and said, "It was a mild one, a mild one. I have no visible residue."

But she knew "residue" was not the right word. Visible signposts, perhaps, a certain look, the way her family inserted one word or two

SHARON WHITE

when they had a chance, the way her little dog looked at her with dis-trust. It all got to be too much. Their loving hands guiding her down stairs, past the homeless curled on sidewalks and motorcycle gangs prowling the boulevards. And then those months of the pandemic. Fights over masks. A woman beaten up in the CVS near their house.

They went to a place in the North one winter soon after her stroke and stayed in an inn where the sheets were very white and they left chocolate on your bed at night. So sweet. They ate in the dining room and she brought her little white dog with her. Piaf slept under the table, and she could see other holidaymakers snatching looks at her from their beautifully set tables.

There were people singing in another room and lights twinkling in the trees outside. Her husband and sons were happy skiing during the day, and she could sit on the porch in the sun with Piaf and think about nothing, nothing at all. There was no struggle to find any words. She was in the first months of her therapy and it was difficult to say anything. She could hardly smile. Don't worry darling, her husband said, we'll get you back to normal in no time, and she would shake her head. She knew there was no normal around the corner.

Her therapist had Gigi draw a clock and she knew from her face, even if she said that's great Gigi, that's great, she'd somehow gotten it wrong, terribly wrong. She studied flashcards and did homework for what felt like hours. She was instructed to substitute one word for another, but she'd never been much of a poet and isn't that what they did? She used to love to tell stories and she could see the painful look on her younger son's face when they were all silent at the dinner table, her boys back from one college or another. One job or another and it was her husband, who used to be the quiet one, who carried the conversation like a suitcase.

THREE

She had several days before she started teaching in the summer program at the American university, so she went to a garden. She'd admired this garden in books for years. When she was in Japan years ago, she was more interested in the mechanics of love than gardens. A brief affair, a few weeks of doing nothing but rolling around on the floor with her boyfriend in a narrow apartment where everything was miniature. It took her weeks to realize she wasn't in love at all, just enamored by the idea. It was so far away, so far away from the kind of life she normally lived.

And she loved the burning bite of sake and how it made her feel. How loved he made her feel, split off from the self she thought she knew, even if she didn't know what she was capable of doing. She didn't know that later when she had her stroke, years later, she wouldn't know who she was at all and the sorting chambers of her

SHARON WHITE

brain would disintegrate so she couldn't even talk to her dog. Piaf, her little dog with the white paws, who she sometimes thought she loved above all else.

Now she was so far away from the woman she once was. Sometimes she wasn't sure she could feel anything at all. Sometimes her body, even though it seemed quite fine, was someone else's. Those breasts her lover caressed as they slept on the floor in the tiny room no longer her breasts. Her back against the tatami mat. The way she could laugh at anything, anything at all. Her whole life stretched out like a measuring tape. Infinite, charmed. But she left him and went back to the orderly life of one academic degree after another. And then her family, and then the lightning. She wanted this time to be a chance to reclaim some kind of wilderness of spirit. Not so worried all the time that this or that would happen. Not so worried all the time about her husband and sons.

It was a garden of Waka poetry. The paths circled the pond in the middle of the garden like a magic incantation. Each viewing spot was a bell. A way to inspire memory. A key to the locked room where the words lived. Precious Seaweed Shore. Her days at the Cape with her mother and father and her brothers and sister. The days burning to a crisp on the sand, cold as hell in the water. Those hours playing in the brook that went down to the sea, the horseshoe crabs moving so slowly along the bottom, waving their blunt spears back and forth. Her brothers stoning the rabbit to death one day when they were visiting cousins two towns away.

Ebb Tide Harbor, her life now.

It took her months before she could draw the clock on the blank piece of paper correctly. And years before she felt confident enough to lecture again. Now she watched a man measure bamboo stakes precisely, and then saw them off, and then hammer them with a wooden mallet into the ground along the edge of the lake. He measured three times and then cut. She watched him happily. She was definitely happy, sitting on the wooden bench in the old garden. Very old, she knew, early 1700s.

Two of the ponds were gone now, but the impression of the water on the surface of the earth remained.

FOUR

She wanted a resurrection. She knew it was blasphemous to want so much. She wanted to be struck anew with life. Instead, God sent her lightning in her brain. And even if the doctors kept saying she'd be fine, she didn't think this state was fine. She was such a talker. She could talk the ear off anyone, couldn't she? Her sons knew that. And as she traveled more and more with her husband and they could do almost anything they wanted, she had so many stories to tell.

When her mother got sick it was up to them to take care of her, first in her older boy's room and then in the facility down the road. It was the only place in miles with a grove of trees. Her mother didn't care at that point if the two rooms looked out at trees, but Gigi did.

It just seemed too much sometimes. The world was crumbling at the edges. Massive fires, families huddled in makeshift camps on the edge of the Mediterranean, violent storms. And then her mother started to say less and less. A kind of imitation of Gigi's stroke, but much worse. She wouldn't come back from this descent into silence.

She brought her meat sauce in a silver thermos. Morsels of chicken in foil. Beautiful sweet ripe clementines. Armfuls of farmers market flowers. Her mother stopped eating, her mother stopped moving, her mother stopped doing anything at all. And what was there to do? Her mother didn't remember the soap operas she'd spent her life watching or the news at 6:30 or anything, really. Gigi was afraid her mother would forget who her daughter was. But she didn't. Her sister came and stayed with her those last months. Her mother took forever to die. She's just doing it on her own time, the kind nurse from Haiti told her. The books can only tell you the average time.

The average time was two weeks. Her mother wanted ten months and she took it.

FIVE

She'd had a bitter fight with him before she left. Her husband said, "I sacrificed all my waking hours to your rehab, and this is what you want to do now that I've got you back?"

"I was still myself, when you thought I wasn't here," Gigi said. "I was still myself all those hours when you were away. I was with the boys in my heart, wasn't I? I fought hard to get back to what you thought you wanted me to be."

But it was all so dramatic, she thought. The simple thing was there were two of her now. The woman he'd loved for so many years and the one who went away. Went away in her head, all the words mismatched, unavailable for the moment. Not useful.

She wasn't about to give up this prize, a job in Tokyo, after she'd waited over two years for the country to open up again to foreigners.

"You're not the same," he said, "not the same at all if you keep this cockamamie idea in your head and leave us again." He was putting the dishes away, wiping off the water on the tops of the mugs with a towel. She backed away from him.

"I can't believe you said cockamamie," she said and then they started to laugh. He was very funny sometimes and she loved that about him. He closed the dishwasher and ran his hands through his short gray hair.

It was a relief to be somewhere like where she was then. Police everywhere, stationed at subways and street corners and outside of train stations to guide your way. The soft patter of drops, now that the rainy season was warming up. The plum season, a woman in her building told her.

She was not in the same world, but it didn't matter. No one knew who she was before, and she'd gotten the job on her own without the help of her husband or sons or even her little dog, who she missed terribly. She could impersonate the scholar she'd been before everything happened. Someone who wrote about land art like Spiral Jetty in Utah. She was convinced her writing about artist Robert Smithson helped her get this job in a place she always wanted to return to.

She'd taken the train to Taito, a part of the city with twenty temples. Arched wooden temples with deities who might be sympathetic to her. It was kind of Zen to walk slowly around the village on her own through the vast cemeteries and winding streets that were spared war and fire and bombing. The hydrangeas were blooming. Delicate lace, bright blue like the sky. She met a girl with an owl. A pet owl, three months old. A baby, the girl told her. For a few yen, Gigi could pet it. But it was enough to look at the owl as the bird swiveled her head back and forth. The soft whirl of spotted caramel feathers around her face. The owl's deep black eyes shining as she looked into them and the owl didn't flinch. The bird was perfectly calm. There was a world there that was very different from the one she'd fled. Serene, astonishing, filled with peace.

SIX

She talked to a man at a pizza party after the first faculty meeting who told her she should get a car, borrow someone's to go to the big international store at the edge of the city. You could get chairs there, you could get anything really. It was stupid to take a train or a bus there, it didn't make sense. After all, what were cars for, if not to transport people to places where they could buy things, he laughed. He was thin and wore a white tunic over his cotton pants. His hair was as white as his clothes. Everything about him was impermanent, a little foggy. She could hardly hear him when he spoke.

"I'm Richard," he said, holding his hand out to her.

"What do you teach?" She clasped his hand lightly.

"I used to teach physics, but now I teach dance and yoga."

"Like the music of the spheres," she said, "so that makes sense. But a little surprising."

Dance, he told her, was what interested him these days. A free form interpretation of traditional dances. Lots of drums, and chimes, and dipping and twirling. A kind of frenzy that set him off. Propelled into another world.

"I'll blast Kodo on my computer. Several low drumbeats building up to a rhythm. One musician drumming faster and faster."

He started to move slowly in the light streaming through the windows. Moving one arm and then another until his body was a counterpoint to the crescendo of drummers he was imagining. His legs bending and then still. Folding his body up like an origami frog on the floor.

"I feel like I'm disappearing into the sound. My body nothing at all," he said, as he popped up from the floor.

A couple of people glanced over at them and then continued talking as if nothing had happened. Was it something they expected from him?

He leaned in close to her, "And you?"

"An art seminar." She was feeling anxious and was happy when the pizzas arrived, balanced in the arms of two students.

The room was filled with men. There were hardly any women. She followed a man with an umbrella out of the building to an annex across the narrow street up the elevator.

"Are you one of the faculty," she asked, "or a parent?"

And he said quickly, "I'm the CFO."

"You're a big deal, then," she said.

When the door opened, he vanished down a corridor and shut the door.

A woman in the business office opened a brown packet filled with the first edition of Gigi's pay and fanned the money out on the desk in front of her. The solemn faces of someone famous in Japan glared at her from the surface of the gray desk. There were so many shades of gray in the city.

She was making a garden on her balcony with a view of the canal. The space was just big enough for several small pots. She'd bought a passion vine, white with deep blue filaments.

Someone had planted a perennial garden along the paved walkway below. In the morning she could smell cut grass. A woman pushing a bike arrived every other day to weed the garden. The roses were blooming. Wasn't it odd that something as ordinary as a rose was blooming in this quite extraordinary city? A man had a workshop under the bridge past the apartment building where she lived. He was bent over and took his willow broom out from the piles of tools and swept the walkway each morning. When she said hello to him, he bowed and then went on with his task.

She was on an island of concrete in the concrete city. Minato Ward. One man at the faculty meeting told her during the last earthquake everything swayed and then was still. He likes to wear women's clothes, another man told her.

SEVEN

It was the first day of classes. She tapped on the keys of the computer at her desk. Motoko, the Japanese-language instructor in the next cubicle, had filled her desk with stuffed animals. Gigi's favorite was the giraffe. His neck curved over her desk and she smoothed the soft fur every now and then as she worked. It was comforting to be in league with an animal spirit.

It had taken her a couple of days before she introduced herself to Motoko. Whenever Gigi passed her she seemed too busy to talk. She was bent over her computer, her fingers tapping on the keyboard. Her brown hair was twisted in a knot at her neck. Like most of the women in the city, she wore a white blouse with a dark skirt. One day Gigi said hello, even though Motoko was typing.

"I love the giraffe," she said as Motoko looked up.

"He is the best," Motoko said. "Though the others have their good points, too." She smiled and lifted her fingers off the keyboard. "I have all these tests to read, and I have to make an exam for tomorrow. It never ends does it?"

"It's too early in the semester for all this work, isn't it?"

"No, my classes have constant work. The students hate to do it," Motoko said. She smoothed her bangs and smiled.

Motoko's motto for Gigi was "When the cat's away, she should play." She told Gigi that her mother was from a tiny village you could see from the Shinkansen on the way to Kyoto. It was folded into the hills not far outside of Tokyo, after you crossed the big river with concrete banks and a braided delta. There were tea bushes growing on the hillsides. Her mother grew up in a house that was her family's for years. The floors were dark and shiny and the rafters smoky from the fire in the irori.

Her mother had moved to Tokyo in the 80s. She wanted to be a businesswoman. Motoko's family lived on a street with lots of French restaurants and patisseries, near the big temple at the top of the hill. Her house was narrow and dark with a little garden in the back that her mother tended just like a monk, Motoko said.

"I think she missed her village, maybe," she told Gigi. "Though, she loved wearing slim skirts and high heels and rubbing elbows with bigwigs on the trains."

Motoko's father was an artist, which didn't make sense at all. A sculptor. She couldn't understand how her parents got together. They were so different and who could put up with her father for years and years? He was a chain-smoker, and wore paint-stained trousers and a little bib with tools propped up in the pockets, and he hardly ever talked unless he thought it was necessary. His great-grandfather was a famous sword maker who'd saved a whole village from destruction when he made the most beautiful sharp swords for each person and

SHARON WHITE

handed them out for free. They fought together to fend off a terrible demon. Now the village was just a tourist trap on a popular route, though you still had to walk up a steep hill to get there.

When she thought no one was looking, Motoko took a little package of bright red paper out of her pocket and opened it carefully. Then she popped a piece of gum into her mouth and chewed. If she was facing the wall no one would know she was doing anything rude.

EIGHT

If there was a story to tell she couldn't remember it some days. And what of the man with the white hair and the white stones around his throat and the white clothes. Richard. She was surprised at how warm his hand was. The press of his hand against her hand.

He really looked angelic, she thought. Spare, white, robed in the lightest of clothes. A kind of Zen impression of a Catholic angel. His face was gentle. He reminded her of Peter Frampton, a musician she really liked when she was in college.

What was his story, she wondered, as she walked home after class past the Buddhist temple with pots of flowers and small trees shading the walkways, the graveyard on the hill with polished sticks near each stone inscribed with sacred words to help the dead, and then up the road past the Friends School and the sleek modern stucco houses and tiny gardens to the boulevard that led to her apartment. Restaurants with plastic menus posted on the windows sold fried food she could smell as she walked past. Pork and beef. The noodle shops reeked of fish broth.

Whewhen she got to her apartment, her head was spinning. Everything was miniature in her place. The chairs, the lamps, the glasses, the forks. That's what her mother's life was like those last weeks, something that had spread out to several houses and states and countries had shrunk to one room. A bed, a chair, a television her mother didn't watch anymore, a sink, a toilet, a brush.

Sometimes there was music that came out of thin air. Like the words she lost all those years ago. Or was it so long ago?

There were children with yellow hats holding their mothers' hands as Gigi got closer to her building. A monk kneeling in the garden, touching the roses one by one. A man feeding two cats by the canal. Was everything a gesture of something else? Her mother's hand fading in her hand as she watched. Her eyes disappearing. Everything sinking into the white sheet of the bed, until finally even her teeth seemed to have disappeared.

NINE

At one of the temples she visited she put coins at the foot of several minor gods who wore pink caps. They were standing guard along the fence to the temple near their leader, a much larger statue with a pink apron around his neck. There were crows the size of eagles carrying pieces of toast and little birds who darted through the towering trees. She missed her husband. He would have laughed at the pink hats. He was pretty irreverent about everything. She was farther away from him than she'd ever been, and she wondered if she was tempting some kind of fate with this desertion.

But she needed, she thought, to go away for a while. Just a few months to remember who she was before. To remember who she was all those years ago when she first fell in love. Before she was a wife and mother. Before she spent those years in rehab. Everything had been a blur for so many years. Putting one foot in front of the other. Smiling and laughing when she thought nothing was really funny anymore. Sitting like a ghost at the table with her family in the beautiful resort, the snow falling gently outside the dining room as the waiters dressed in costumes from another country removed plate after plate from the table. Nothing was working then. Her face as blank as the tablecloth.

A woman was pushing a cart filled with willow brooms and wooden buckets covered with black calligraphy. For holy water, she thought. Bouquets of fading flowers covered the graves. Why didn't someone take them away once they started dying? Bundles of wires crisscrossed the sky above her head as she walked into a tiny alley where they were selling juice and puffy buns with cream. She hadn't been hungry in such a long time, but the buns were soft and warm in her mouth. It was a relief to be alone. She didn't have to search for the words she wanted. She could let whatever came to the surface be what she wanted to say. Penguin. Pigeon. Parrot.

TEN

M en with white gloves drove the cabs in the city, the seats covered with white lace. They seemed to be driving empty cabs wherever she looked. Sometimes in the morning she saw them pulled up at the curb outside her apartment building. Polishing the mirrors. Were there people she couldn't see in the back seat?

She wondered if ghosts were following her when she went to the 100-yen store where the checkout person, a lively woman, told her there were so many foreigners in the neighborhood now, or took the little local bus to the hills north of where she was living.

She stopped at a bakery on the way home from the university and bought a cookie topped with a cherry. A girl with short purple hair wrapped the sugar cookie in a paper bag and handed it to her, smiling. The steep narrow street wound up the hill past two temples and onto a shaded road beside a park. She sat on one of the wooden benches

SHARON WHITE

under a tree bent with green fruit and crumbled pieces of the cookie for the birds pecking at the grass. She'd forgotten to eat lunch and chewed the half of the cookie she'd kept for herself.

She was thinking about the book she'd been reading. Motoko had given her a collection of accounts about the tsunami after the 3/11 earthquake in Tohoku, translated into English. Information to encourage escape and fortitude when the next big earthquake happened. Many people who survived said it got dark and started to snow, cold and silent. Everyone remembered the silence. In one place, a gold wall of water filled the alley at the end of a city street.

A restaurant owner didn't find his wife for three days but she was fine. She talked to her baby, unborn, kicking. Snow falling on everything. Her husband said he knew it wasn't an ordinary earthquake since he couldn't keep standing. It was much more violent.

Another woman was playing mahjong. Her body was tossed up and the mahjong tiles flew away. Soaking wet, she tied herself to a boat. She said, rather than being scared, she was overcome with a sense of shock—the shock of having seen what was unimaginable before.

When she was watching her mother die all those months, her dog came with her. Piaf waited for morsels of food Gigi's mother dropped on the rug, or the crumbs from the tiny pieces of bread her mother ate. One day her dog noticed something on the ceiling. Her younger son was visiting. He said he thought it was angels.

She laughed, "Really?" she asked. "I didn't think you believed in any of that stuff."

"Mom," he said, laughing, "look at the way Piaf's acting."

She was definitely acting strange circling her mother's hospital bed, sniffing under the covers, whining at the ceiling. It was comforting, in a way, that angels were there to help her mother, when no one had been around when Gigi had her stroke.

She was making lunch, leftovers heated up in a pan. A strange thing to do, but there it was. She usually ate yogurt. A plate was in her hand. She was walking across the kitchen, past the white jars arranged on the shelves, and the shining silver refrigerator, and then she fell. Lightning and then nothing.

When she could see again she dragged herself across the kitchen floor to the hallway and then to the living room. Her phone was on a table in the middle of the room. It took her hours to reach the phone and when she got through to her husband all she could do was make a noise, a simple noise she thought sounded like help me, but her husband said much later, months later, was more like a croak.

ELEVEN

One of her students, Sunil, a solemn boy from India, told her he almost died climbing Fuji. You were supposed to be able to see it from the city, a perfectly shaped cone with snow on the top. But she'd been lost in the concrete caverns for days now and couldn't understand how you could see the mountain from Tokyo. It rose up, she knew, from the plains below.

He was climbing the mountain with six friends. They were ill-equipped and cold by the time they got to the shoulder of the mountain. There was a hut where they paid a huge amount to sleep on hard pillows and wrap themselves in one thin blanket. He was not feeling well. Maybe it was the altitude, he thought, and his friends wanted to give up. But he went ahead in time to see the sunrise. He was so tired, he told her, that he slipped at the edge of a ravine and was almost never heard from again. And he was so young. His mother would have been bereft and his friends very unhappy, but he caught himself and they all went on to reach the top. It took them eighteen hours to climb the mountain.

She was thinking perhaps she should tell Richard that she'd take him up on his offer to rent a car and drive to the big international store. She wanted to go somewhere, anywhere out of the city beyond the concrete buildings. Was there something wrong with that? She wanted to go to the prefecture with the wild boar. She'd started to read *The Japan Times*, where one of her students was an intern. Deer and boar were eating grain and fruit on the abandoned farms. She'd seen a picture of it in the newspaper. Thousands of wild boar with blunt noses and fierce eyes. They'd come down from the mountains. They were comfortable in the towns and had plenty of food.

It was ironic they were survivors, and yet hundreds of hunters had tracked them down and killed as many as they could. The government was encouraging some of the people in the evacuation zone who'd fled their cities and villages years ago to return. What was it like to go back to a place scoured by water and fire and radiation? How could you begin your life again after everything you knew had disappeared? Your husband, your home, your rice field, your horse. What was it like to live when the person you loved had died? How could you survive this?

In a way it was so much like Smithson's ideas about art. How his sculptures like Spiral Jetty changed over time. How the basalt rocks, and salt crystals, and mud disappeared under the waters of the Great Salt Lake and then reappeared years later. It was difficult to understand the work as a whole, unless you saw it from a plane.

Her husband had been calling her, trying to convince her to come home. "You can use your health," he said, "as an excuse. Tell them you didn't realize how stressful the trip would be."

"But I'm fine," she said. "And I don't want to come home yet. Classes have barely started. This is important to me even if you think it's stupid."

"I'm not important to you?" he asked. It was his night and her morning. There was no way they could talk about this. It was yesterday there and today here. They were not even on the same globe, somehow.

She turned the heat up on the stove under a big pot to boil spaghetti. And then she filled a jug with water. It was soothing to tend her collection of plants on the tiny balcony. Her passion vine was growing along the metal latticework. There were several buds now on the plant. She looked down at the canal flowing in and out of the bay, once barricaded against foreign ships. The water was foaming at the outfall pipe, sparkling in the lights along the path.

Her long rehab had seemed like it would never end, but she was passionate about being able to talk again. And she did, but not in the way she thought she would. She was thinking she wanted to see the wild boar.

TWELVE

The elevator door opened at her floor and Richard appeared. It was such a small elevator that you had to stand one in front of the other to fit in.

She laughed as he backed up and gestured to her. She leaned away from him clutching her tote full of papers. They had three floors to go before they reached the lobby.

"This is funny," she said. "You live here too?"

"Yes. On the eleventh floor."

"But not so weird."

"No," he smiled. "There are a lot of people hidden away in these apartments. How do you like living in our building?"

"I like it," she said. "I like being right above the canal."

"I don't notice it as much from the eleventh floor. But I'm happy I have the balcony. It's my lifesaver in case of a disaster, a ladder folded

30   SHARON WHITE

up in a box."

"I've been thinking," she said, "that I'd like to go to the big store to get a chair for the balcony."

"Sure," he said. "I'm free tomorrow in the afternoon. I'll rent a car."

"I'll pay," she said.

"No, don't worry. I want to stock up on toilet paper."

"Toilet paper?" She laughed.

"It's a lot cheaper at the big store. Meet in the lobby at two?"

Now here she was. The window down. He said he liked it that way. Her hair was blowing in the wind and he was driving her to the big store. The bright yellow rental car zipping along the crowded highway as fast as he could go. She didn't have an international driver's license, so she was stuck in the passenger's seat.

It was almost as bad as when her father drove when she was young. She used to squeeze down in the back seat, almost to the floor. He drove like a madman, so fast she was convinced she'd die right there on the narrow road above the Pacific. Waves breaking apart below her. Now she was with another fast driver on the other side of the same ocean, turned around in time.

He was curious, he said, about the numbers of radioactive boar in the exclusion zone in Fukushima. He'd read a paper by a biologist who studied gray wolves in the Red Forest at Chernobyl. There were some adverse effects on wildlife from radiation, but humans were more destructive for the wolves. Humans had destroyed so much it made sense that animals would carve an eco-niche out of habitat that was toxic. Cesium-137 in the boar was 300 times higher than the safe limit for human consumption, but the radioactive material didn't seem to affect the animals. Several expensive restaurants in the city listed wild boar or *botan* as a delicacy on their menus. They advertised it as *botan nabe*. Wild boar hotpot.

"I've been thinking about those animals in Chernobyl," Gigi said. "How amazing it is they survived. I knew someone who lived over the border in Norway. I was afraid his sheep would get sick."

"I went with my friend Hiroshi to Tohoku about a month after the disaster," Richard said, turning away from the road for a second to look at her. And even though it was just a moment, she was startled by the spark she felt. It was something she didn't expect. A brief ripple in the air. It doesn't mean anything at all, she thought, nothing at all.

"You'd better keep your eyes on the road," she said.

He laughed. "I used to race cars for fun."

She glanced out the window. Sun was glinting off the cars, flashing against her eyes as they sped by in the fast lane.

"My friend felt guilty he'd escaped the horror. He'd been away at a party for a colleague when the first tremors hit. A celebration. Hiroshi wanted to see what had happened. His parents had a spinach farm in the prefecture, and by that time their whole crop was off limits. He hadn't been able to talk to them until weeks after everything happened.

"We took the highway first. It runs along the train tracks. A Shinkansen had nosedived into a gorge along the coast. Buildings just crumbled steel. Reclaimed land liquefied. Only the Tori gates of some of the shrines were standing. And blackbirds everywhere, crows and ravens and vultures. For miles we didn't see any gulls at all. They'd disappeared. Fishing villages were gone. Boats hauled up on the streets.

"Kids in the cities wore face masks, and later they were evacuated once the readings of radiation levels went up. Traffic lights worked in some villages where everyone had disappeared. One cop waved us through on the empty beach road. My friend couldn't let his guilt go, and it got worse and worse as we drove closer to the epicenter. The cherry trees were blooming all over the prefecture. Hiroshi stopped to get cigarettes a couple of times and we saw surgical facemasks piled on shelves. We passed a vending machine selling bottles of sparkling water, soda and beer standing along the side of the road with nothing else around it."

"That's so tragic," she said. "How's your friend doing now?"

"Still guilty. Still mourning, but better. It's impossible to imagine it. Here we are."

He took the exit off the highway and turned into the parking lot of the big store.

THIRTEEN

Sometimes this city felt like the movie *Blade Runner* and sometimes it felt like a miracle. The streets near the harbor torn up with construction, the salty smell of the pavement near the fish market. Men with swirling tattoos on their arms and legs shifted boxes into trucks. But some neighborhoods appeared as if they were dreams. Little wooden houses with pointed roofs, pots of flowers in the tiny alleys, flowered fabric for sale in shop windows. Old women bent over their cats, setting out food.

She understood the geography of the city as a loop. She imagined the places she traveled to on the Yamanote Line as spokes out from the tracks. That's what it felt like when she boarded the train and it sped past apartments with laundry drying on hangers, or futons draped over railings, or the neon signs covering the sides of massive buildings, or electric signs flashing as the train passed clusters of pine trees with

SHARON WHITE

pointed tops, or camellias in bloom on the edges of the tracks.

She liked thinking about the gardens she was visiting as a kind of land art with some of the same concerns as Smithson's work. The land as sculpture. She had an idea for an essay, something that seemed to be building in her mind. Tentative. But still, the words appearing one after the other.

The garden she'd gone to in the morning was in the courtyard of a sculptor's house. The façade looked like a Bauhaus design painted black, but the actual house was traditional, built around a garden of the most beautiful stones from all over the country. A large smooth stone from the north, other stones covered in lichen from the forests set in the pond, filled again and again with the clearest water.

Spouts of water bubbled out from carved stones. Koi, some 100 years old, swam back and forth as she watched the water flow. Awakening, the whole garden was an awakening and that's what she wanted to do. Even though she was quite old and damaged in more ways than one.

In another garden, she saw an iris field that was once a rice paddy to train the children of samurai families about the hardships of rice cultivation. Or, at least, that's what she was told. Wasn't it important for everyone to learn about the hardships of cultivation? Everyone around her on the trains or buses seemed to be only aware of things, the value of purchases folded neatly in their bags.

FOURTEEN

She was trying to sleep more, but it was like sleeping at high altitude. Fitful. Full of disturbing dreams about her mother and father. She'd dreamed her father was standing in her room when she came out of the shower and handed her a kimono. She grabbed a towel.

"What are you doing, Dad?"

"When did you get those?" he asked, pointing to her breasts.

"Ages ago," she said. "You shouldn't be here."

He was dressed in shorts and a polo shirt. About to play golf. "It's great in heaven," he said, "but I miss you kids."

She didn't want to ask him if he was with Mom. Too much information, she thought. Or if he'd already met some bimbo and was having the time of his life with a blonde bombshell. Someone not at all like Mom. She was awake in a split second and left only with trying to figure out how old she was when he died. Surely old enough to have breasts.

Things were like that now. Her brain not as sharp, she thought, as it was before the lightning, before that afternoon when lunch became something else. Of course she was much older when her father died. She had at least one son, and she loved her son above all else. She was consumed with her family. She didn't have time for whatever was going on with her mother and father. She was working, she was taking her son to daycare, she was making meals for her husband who suddenly was a big wheel. His second book was important. He was giving talks all over the world. Everything was a swirl of activity. She was wondering if she would ever remember what it was like to be herself again. Solitary, ambitious.

She'd gone to the Museum of Contemporary Art across the street from the Imperial Palace the day before. She wanted some time just looking at things. Things that had been made by solitary people who thought a lot. There was a room filled with Robert Smithson's notes and objects connected to Spiral Jetty. She'd driven out once with her husband and two boys almost to the place where they could see the sculpture just underwater in the Great Salt Lake, but the road was a mess, and they'd run out of time so they turned around at Promontory Point. They would have missed their plane back home. She'd wanted for years to see Spiral Jetty.

It was strange Smithson died in a plane crash in Texas. He was so young, thirty-five, almost around the age of her older son. And he was looking at a site for another earthwork. A track of red rocks curving on the desert outside Amarillo. It was there now, she'd seen pictures. Nancy Holt, his widow, and other artists completed the work near the place he died. Smithson picked disrupted sites, so his work was part of renewal and rebirth. Amarillo Ramp once balanced in the water, irrigation for cattle, but now curved in the dip where the water once was.

She was not paying attention to the whole room in the museum, the room where there were those objects connected with Spiral Jetty.

A film of water, a box with crumbled pieces of paper, a map from that dry country. So she was surprised when she felt something under her foot as she stepped back from the images of water, the sound of Smithson's voice. A voice from another country, another world, the time before her lightning. Guards moved swiftly to her side and she looked down and saw that she was just about to step on a still life of rocks in a brown cardboard container in the shape of an L.

FIFTEEN

She woke every morning with all her molecules lit. That's what it felt like. Her body was more alive than it had felt in years. And what about that frisson when Richard glanced at her as they sped along the highway? She laughed and began to sing "just a little crush." All she could remember of the song was that piece of the chorus, and she felt the hot air in Florida when she used to drive her mother's station wagon on the back road along the wild edges of the canal, and sing it at the top of her lungs and feel that thrill. She was young then, she was a little in love, she was driving really fast in the big car on the narrow sandy road, and nothing could touch her.

It was such a long time before she could put a sentence together after her stroke. Her therapist had sheet after sheet of exercises for her to do. Filling in sentences like a fourth grader. Dredging up grammar from the depths of her brain. Sometimes it felt like there was nothing there anymore. No word for key, or apple, or car. The trick was to search for nearby words that might give someone else some idea of what she wanted to say. It was a game. A trick. A way to pretend she was normal.

She stopped teaching. It was difficult enough to remember the word for son or husband, let alone plinth or column. But here she was teaching art history to ten students from all over the world, really. In the city for one reason or another.

"It's such a short course," she said to her husband and sons. "I'll just be away for a couple of months."

"That's a joke, Mom," her older son said. "You'll be most of the way around the world."

"You're so bored with us you want to get that far away?" Her husband asked and laughed. He was stirring sauce on the stove. Her younger boy was setting the table. Jobs she once did without thinking. They were celebrating her adventure, even though they were reluctant to let her go for so long.

Weeks after her stroke, when the occupational therapist had her make tomato sauce, she couldn't remember how to use a spoon and picked up the smallest knife to stir the pot. One day her older son found her brushing her ear with her toothbrush. "It would help, Mom," he said, gently taking the electric toothbrush out of her hand, "if you used this on your teeth."

This interchange of one thing for another was maybe not so bad. Why did it matter anyway? In this country you used chopsticks.

She sat on a low white leather couch creased with age in her apartment and rode an escalator to the grocery store where she found the same kind of cookies they had at home and fruit swaddled like expensive glassware with pink and green hats. Everything she unwrapped from the store was like a gift.

When she walked along the canal, she saw men sitting on the benches before they went to their offices. Their eyes closed, leaning back, the white heron who had a nest near one of the bridges slicing past them in the air. One man bent over his dark trousers fanning his legs with a paper fan spread wide, picking lint off the dark fabric. Another squatted down, feeding two gray cats crouched by the edge of a building.

The roses struggled now in the gardens, but zinnias and poppies were starting to bloom. Something smelled bitter. Like tomato leaves.

On her way to the university she passed a shrine. She could hear a monk beating a drum with a stick, a ringing sound that filled her with peace.

SIXTEEN

She was lost. She'd turned left instead of right on her way home from the university. She was trying to get her bearings when she saw a Starbucks. Richard was standing outside talking to someone she didn't know. She didn't want him to read anything in her face. She didn't want to admit she'd thought about kissing him after being so close to him in the car.

He motioned to her.

"I'm just about to have a cup of tea. Want to join me?"

"Tea would be great," she said. "The trip to the store was fun."

"A little different, isn't it? You get to see more of the city. How's the class going?" He asked as they sat down at a table near the door. It was too clean for a Starbucks. There were several people who she'd seen at the university sitting at the small tables. The coffee machine hissed.

"Fine, but it's early."

"Too early, I suppose, to really know."

"Yes," she laughed.

"You're settling in?" He asked.

"Yes, I'm visiting more gardens. I never have a chance to do this at home. I'm thinking about writing something on land art. The gardens as sculpture. My husband can't stand wandering around in gardens unless there's something to eat somewhere."

"A practical guy," Richard said. But it seemed like he ate hardly anything at all.

And then he was telling her about a sand garden in the ancient capital. He said the shogun, tired of war and famine and pestilence, made a house above the city. He only thought of art.

"Like you," she said. "Abandoning science for dance."

"You might have something there."

The garden was sand, still there now. Ridged sand built up in one spot with a truncated pyramid where the shogun looked at the moon. The carefully raked sand garden at the foot of the palace, the waves in the sand meant to remind us of the ocean, of time, of persistent motion. The place was called the Silver Palace, though the shogun never finished painting the temple with silver flecks.

He said, "You should really go and see it. There's a serpentine design around a lake with rocks from all over the shogun's feudal kingdom. Each one with a name."

He'd just come back from Kyoto and on the way home he saw a woman in the train station. He'd seen her first getting on the train in Kyoto, but noticed her again in the station. Her face turned to the left. She was glittering with a cluster of diamonds in her ear and she was standing alone, even though her husband and son were near her.

"She seemed so lost," he said. "Her son kept trying to touch her wrist and she pulled it away. She had a tiny diamond bracelet on. Everything about her was silver. Silver sweater to her ankles, silver clasp on her earring. The way she turned away from her husband who held his kid's hand tightly."

Richard was so different from her husband. She watched as he squeezed his teabag and put it on a tiny white saucer. He was almost too tall to sit comfortably in the small chair. He was hunched over the table.

Children were pouring out of the building across the street. She missed her sons, though they hadn't been that age for years. She used to love reading to them, all the picture books spread around her as they sat on the futon in her workroom.

Richard's hands were old hands, she thought, though his face was unlined. She picked up her cup. The tea was cold already.

The Starbucks was emptying. Students shuffling their bags onto their shoulders. She saw a woman she recognized carefully pushing her chair under the table.

That morning she'd walked against the flow of workers racing through the train station. It was pouring and she wanted to take a bus to school. She had to wait a few minutes until she could wade through the bodies, all dressed in white and black. White and black in variations all around her. Their faces blank and cold.

Richard sipped his tea and said, "I went to the place where Koetsu, the artist, lived when he was old. It was very beautiful up in the hills. He had a whole village there of artists."

He told her it was inspiring. He sat on the bench against the wall of the smallest teahouse, the place where Koetsu had died. Koetsu called the house where he lived the hut of great emptiness. "That's what we all want isn't it? To achieve emptiness, the mind as blank as sand. The world just going in and out, in and out, until there's no feeling."

He picked up his cup and sipped the last of his tea. "I didn't think about much except how peaceful it was. The smell of the pines was like being in the mountains when I was a kid."

Gigi felt terrified for an instant thinking about her mind as blank as sand. She'd struggled so long to erase that minute when there was nothing. And it was such a long struggle for so many years, she told Richard. Each morning she'd practice the words she'd remembered from the day before. It was a game she played when her husband was still asleep. She'd go out to their small courtyard where the robins were whistling, and it was still quiet. Too early for the buses that shook their house. And then she was embarrassed she'd told him anything at all.

"Meditation helps," he said. "Not to relax you so much, but for the practice. Zazen, sitting. Just sitting."

He told her he'd gotten used to seeing menus with horsemeat in the city, but he didn't like it. There were lots of things he didn't like, but he tried to not think about them. He couldn't just let them go, even though he knew it was the only way to achieve anything like enlightenment. Like the way he felt after his first sesshin. Outside of himself, nicer, not as riled by things. He was the only lay person at the monastery. His job was to feed the chickens scratching the dirt near a red and gold painted coop. Tourists passed by on their way into the mountains. He wondered if it was significant that feeding the chickens exposed him to strangers every day. It might have been part of his training. The pilgrims were all on different paths to enlightenment.

SEVENTEEN

The city presses down around her after her days in the foreign country. Ambulances politely calling out to pedestrians to please move away from the vehicle, the women in the department store showing her all the attributes of the pillow she wants to buy anyway. They instruct her to try it out, her head on a piece of gauze covering the pillow, her feet placed on a sheet of plastic at the foot of the bed. When the transaction is finished, the two women, dressed in matching tailored clothes like a uniform, bow and thank her over and over again.

It's the time of the year when trains are delayed in the city. The electric screens in the subway announce passenger injury several times a day. Or antelope on the tracks. Gigi thinks it's a problem with translation. Could there really be antelope in this country? The term passenger injury means someone has jumped, several people at the faculty meeting told her. It's a bad time of year for that. The rainy season coming up, the brutality of late spring. Everything blossoming. New life.

She teaches Tuesday and Thursday and goes into the office on Friday for office hours. When she's anxious it's harder to call up the words she wants.

Gigi knew she was lucky, even after her stroke she knew it could have been much worse. Even as she sat in the inn at the ski resort, her face a mask, her husband and sons skiing through the woods, she knew she was lucky to be there and not in some limbo. But that didn't erase the bitterness that it had happened at all.

Most of her colleagues are wound up in their work. She knew how easy it was to burn yourself out.

R ichard told her he stands on his balcony at night mesmerized by the lights. He gets a charge from being so far away from everything in a place where the living and the dead share space with each other. Rub elbows in the trains, eat their lunch together in the little parks tucked between the buildings. Sweep the walkways with their willow brooms and cart the shriveled flowers away from the graves. Feed the fish in the lotus pond in the park at the zoo, the pink flowers opening above the dark leaves. He'd gone to Ueno a few days before and there was a man feeding tiny bird after tiny bird from his hand. There were signs of generosity all over the city if you looked closely. Nothing like the grasping nature of most people in the U.S. Why would he ever want to go back to that? He wished he'd been in the country when it just opened to the West. That would be cool.

"You know the movie *The Last Samurai*?"

"My kids liked it," she said.

He said he secretly liked the escapades of Tom Cruise and the rest of the samurai as they fought against the forces of the modern world.

Her students are hard to read, quiet and polite, so she hardly ever has to answer questions. She shows movies and slides in elaborately constructed PowerPoints. Her husband had helped her put things together before she left. She just walks herself through the information on the slides and points out the important details of whatever piece of art she's talking about and everything goes smoothly.

"Just follow the words on the PowerPoint and you'll be fine," he said. "They don't know the difference between a portico and a plinth, so it won't matter if you mess up now and then."

She knew she didn't tell her husband enough how much she loved him. That was the problem, wasn't it? She was afraid he'd wake up some morning and realize he had poured so much wine into her chalice and all she did was drink and drink and never distribute the goods to the congregation. She didn't say thank you enough for the hours he spent drilling her on vocabulary or taking her up and down the corridor in rehab until she could walk straight and not list to the side. Until she could get up off the floor on her own and the therapist said she might be ready to go home.

At the Cape when she was young, not so young, just after she graduated from college, she would visit her aunt and uncle and stay in a bedroom in the basement. Right on a marsh. She was depressed, silent. She wasn't sure who she was, what she wanted to be. The marsh smelled like eggs at low tide. Herons poked their beaks into the mud.

It was the light that called her to the ocean. A brilliant glitter on the waves, the salt spray on her tongue in the morning. The local peaches were ripe and she ate one large peach for breakfast each day.

The peach was as big as a grapefruit.

Now, every morning, she wakes to bright light, almost burning. She'd been hollowed out, she realized. So determined to get better. Her body disappearing under desire that wasn't really desire but a kind of willing everything to go back to the way it was. She still hadn't caught up to what she wanted. How she wanted to be able to breathe again and be touched without feeling like it was a waste of time. The way she was all body so many years ago when she first visited Japan, her skin itchy from the tatami mat.

She reads in the news that pigeons have been arrested for carrying little backpacks with pills sewn into the fabric. The backpacks are miniature and fashioned to look like their feathers. The pigeons don't know they're drug mules. They just love to fly.

EIGHTEEN

Gigi was with some colleagues at a restaurant near the university that served beef. Her first full week of classes was over. Kenichi, who grew up in South Africa, was telling her about a woman, a woman blown out to sea who kept her calm.

She floated all the way from an isolated island to Norway, he said. Two days in a little boat and the woman was fine, perfectly fine, though her sons thought she was probably dead and her dog, one of those black and white sheep dogs, kept barking and whining all night for two nights. She was quite fine, like most of the women on the island who did much of the work because their menfolk were off in small boats catching herring for companies that didn't care at all about the men or the women or the children.

Someone said, pass me your glass, Gigi, and I'll fill it. She knew she shouldn't be drinking wine, but she was, and that her doctor had told her one small glass was okay, but that was it. So she was flaunting fate. Was that the right word? Like the woman in the little boat who floated out of her life and then back two days later. She could be lost forever.

The yakiniku restaurant was hot and crowded. They'd been taking turns cooking their pieces of steak on a coal grill.

One of the instructors, who had a cubicle near hers, told her it was complicated for a woman in Japan. She was an American married to a Japanese man. She'd spent the last year in Paris and when she came back she had to get acclimated again to life in the prefecture. Another told her she'd had two children for the country.

"It's what we do," she said and laughed. "That's why there are so many women on electric bikes taking their children to school."

Gigi's neighborhood was full of those women careening on bikes with little motors, racing down the sidewalks, sure that everyone would get out of the way. The bikes always had two seats, one for a child in the front and another for a child in the back. But she couldn't complain about any of that. She'd had two children, too, even though she went back to work as soon as she could. These women stayed home with their children and wore beautifully tailored clothes in muted colors.

They were so polite and so distant sometimes she thought she would scream. She wished Motoko had come with them to the restaurant, but she'd headed home to spend the night with her mother who was having a bad day.

She wasn't sure if she was breaking some rules in the way she dressed or how she gazed at someone as she walked in the city. She realized as it got warmer, her T-shirts were probably too low cut. When she said good morning to a man in the tiny elevator in her building, he giggled. A man on the bus turned and stared at her. She was afraid to go into the tiny restaurants near the train station alone where she saw men and women bent over their bowls of noodles. This was unfamiliar territory.

And she was haunted by her mother who had hardly worked a day in her life. A woman who wore beautiful clothes and had her hair done every week. Who commandeered the room and set the table just so. And then her mother stopped eating and drinking and talking. Who knew what the women were thinking who blasted by her on the sidewalks as she walked back to her apartment from the university. The women in her art seminar wanted more than that. Or at least that's what they told her. Who could really believe what anybody said? Sometimes people wanted something very different from what they told you they really truly wanted. Who knew that, after the last few years, she would want to leave her husband at home and travel halfway around the world?

"We all miss you," her husband said when she spoke to him after the party. The line was so clear, as if they were talking in the kitchen standing close to each other as he sautéed the chicken and popped the cork on a bottle of white wine. He was such a good cook. And such a thoughtful man. Why was she angry at him now and then for nothing? Nothing at all.

"But do you miss me as much as you thought you would, or is this all a game?"

"Not a game for me," he said, "I'm sick with worry about you, but didn't want to tell you that. I thought you'd blow up at me."

"How many times have I blown up at you?" She asked.

"Hmm. Not many, I guess," and then he laughed.

NINETEEN

She put her armful of garden books on the checkout desk in the library. She had so much time to herself. She could almost imagine that she hadn't lived another life at all. That life where her husband and sons and little dog lived. She had no attachment to them now that they were so far away. Everything was so odd and stirring that there wasn't room for how she felt about the people she thought she loved. No room for missing. Wasn't that strange? Instead of being afraid, she was awake.

The last time she'd been so passionate about Japanese gardens was in college. She'd thought she might become a landscape architect. The authors discussed everything from the expansive gardens of samurai to the tiny courtyard gardens of merchants in Kyoto.

The librarian's gray hair was pulled into a tight ponytail at his neck. He went through the books one by one, holding each cover under the scanner.

"How are things going?" he asked.

She wasn't sure how to answer. She'd been surprised the day before by a student who stopped her as she was going up the stairs. She was on her way to eat lunch in her assigned cubicle. He wasn't much taller than she was, but he was built like a wrestler. His blond hair was clipped short. His arms were covered in tattoos. Her forehead started to throb. She was tempted to push him down the stairs.

"You're on the wrong side going up here. It's different than in the states. You can't just carry your privileged shit the way you do there," he said, and then he let her pass. She wondered if he was just angry or it was something about her face. Reserved, placid. Maybe she just rubbed him the wrong way. She was always a little to the left or right in this beautiful country. Never sure what side of the path she should walk on or which way was correct on the stairs. She'd hoped she could lose that sense of misdirection she'd had at home ever since her stroke. Things rearranged, disrupted, out of balance.

Gigi said, "I met a student on the stairs yesterday. Blond, short, older, lots of tattoos. He said some weird things to me."

The librarian said, "Don't let him bother you. It's best to ignore him. Don't engage. Mike's an American from Iowa. One of the students who's been in the service. He was sent to Iraq as support for a Navy SEAL unit. He had a bad time there."

He told her she needed to chill out and go to an ancient garden on the bay, Hama-rikyu. "I went there," he said, "not long ago and it was nice, lots of trees. You could smell salt water. It's not far away from where you live. And you'll pass a famous Shinto shrine on the way."

He seemed to have something hidden, she thought, some kind of tension under his skin. He must work out to have such hidden splendor, but that's not what she thought at all. For years she couldn't remember the word splendor and then she did. It was like magic to be connected to these words again.

"You know about Shinto?" He asked her, leaning his elbows on the counter.

"Just a bit."

"People's lives are always intertwined with nature in Japan. Shinto defines a god as anything virtuous and superior to humans. Sun, water, trees. The word for shrine originally meant woods and the word for garden, *niwa*, meant the gathering place of gods. At Ise Jingu, the traditional shrine of the imperial family, you can see an early sacred courtyard, a place where worshippers connect to the realm beyond time and space. The white gravel's not just empty space."

The very early gardens were designed, he told her, to attract kami, powerful spirits. They were sacred places on stony beaches or in the forest marked off with a rice-fiber rope and covered with pebbles.

"It's a place of pure presence. *Yuniwa*. Space set aside and purified for kami."

W as her brain working better now that she was in this country full of gardens, so far away? She flicked off her shoes inside her apartment and pattered on the floor barefoot. The impure dirt left at the door. The sacred within her house. She knew one thing, she might be getting a little dopey. Sentimental, full of Broadway songs, just like when she was eight and danced Sunday away listening to *My Fair Lady* in the basement.

Everything wasn't perfect in the ancient country. Men smoked alone behind a fence of bushes on the overpass to the trains. Silent, furtive. And those mornings on her walk along the canal when she saw salarymen who'd had too much to drink the night before and were wound up in a ball.

There was a man who seemed to spend all his nights on a bench near the end of the path. He was thin, too thin for the pants and jacket he wore, a green uniform with an insignia. In the morning he was surrounded by cans. The swampy smell of the harbor mixing with stale beer. Maybe he was homeless.

She missed the famous shrine on the way to the garden. This part of the city was torn up with construction. Nothing was where it was supposed to be, according to the map. When she found the ancient garden she was relieved.

It had started to rain, light invisible drops. They tapped on her umbrella as she unfurled it near the entrance. She paid the admission fee and the docent handed her a map. A wooden bridge led to a teahouse in the middle of a lake, covered in wisteria.

She was thinking about the wooden shrines at Ise in an ancient cryptomeria forest, dismantled and reconstructed in a twenty-year cycle on an identical lot, adjacent to the present shrines. The librarian had explained that the shrines are immortal. *Kami* are drawn to the space intermittently connecting time and space. *Ma*, pregnant with meaning, waiting for an event to happen.

The garden was full of very old pine trees, supported by polished poles. They were too heavy for their own good, but impressive. One pine was 300 years old, planted by the sixth shogun when he redesigned the garden. The trees around the lake had lived for hundreds of years and escaped the fires burning all around the garden during the last war.

She was far beyond the path where she usually walked. Water from the bay was channeled into the lake.

The rich, and there were quite a few of these families, used to come to trap ducks in the lake, she read on the map. They would feed them grain and then catch them with nets. A mean trick, she thought. Now there were women and men dressed like warriors. They carried their bamboo bows and arrows in a long canvas bag, slung on their shoulders.

She walked slowly around the perimeter of the garden until she got to a mound covered with grass near the place where the river met

SHARON WHITE

the bay. This was a grave to console the spirits of the ducks who'd died.

She was surprised to see the student who'd blocked her way on the stairs. He was sitting on a bench looking out at the water. It was weird. She saw him pick up something small and dark and hold it to the side of his head. Was it a gun? She walked quickly closer to him and was about to call out when he turned and she could see it was a pair of binoculars. The rain had stopped and the sun was breaking through the clouds. She would never have imagined he would come here.

She waved at him, and he put the binoculars down and nodded his head. She walked toward him. He patted the bench and she sat down.

"Have you seen the white heron?" she asked.

"Not yet. Soon, probably. Sometimes he's like clockwork. Hey, I'm sorry I was an idiot the other day."

"You scared me a bit, but I've had worse," she said and smiled. "I'm Gigi."

"Mike."

He told her he'd done all he could for the country and now look at him. Addicted to pain killers, scrounging around for a job. Stuck in school again with brats who could hardly think straight and had parents who were willing to pay a load of money to guarantee they had good jobs.

"What the fuck," Mike said, "my parents didn't give a shit about me. That's why I ended up here. I enlisted right out of high school."

He said he'd been in the service for twenty years and lived near the U.S. base in Yokosuka. Now he was taking advantage of the GI bill to get a job in business. He was a chief, in charge of the guns, and had married a Japanese girl.

"And you know what they're like. She wants to fit in even though she's married to a gaijin. She wants to have kids, but I'm not sure. Who wants to have kids in this world?"

He'd grown up in Iowa right on a corn field and was probably filled with chemicals from all the spraying they did. He couldn't smell ammonia without thinking of the miles and miles of fields drenched with fertilizer. His parents' house was one of those tiny boxes lined up in a row along the fields. His dad drank too much and his mother was silent much of the time, counting the minutes until her kids left the house and she could do nothing.

"If you need another class, you can still add mine," she said. "I'm a really easy A."

"Thanks, I'm all set. I'm taking dance with Richard. Don't laugh," he said as she smiled. "He's a pretty chill guy."

"Very chill," she said and got up. "See you."

"Yeah, see you."

She turned back toward the tea house, the sun flashing on her face as she walked across the wooden bridge. The wisteria smelled sickly sweet, like Lik-M-Aid candy from when she was young.

TWENTY

She met her new boss again in the street when she was looking for somewhere to buy lunch. He was pushing a bike. A young woman, very pretty, was trailing behind. Richard had told her he didn't mind it that his boss was a prick. The dean left Richard alone. Perhaps because he didn't complain about the size of his classes or teaching night courses. He stayed off committees. Left it to the dean to rub elbows with his international pals in the neighborhood. The embassies were filled with officials who wanted a job for their partners.

"How are you?" Gigi asked.

"Great. I'm going to work out and she's going home. You know they're here to review me at the university. I thought I'd look for a putter. When those meetings are taking place on Friday, I'll be playing golf with Fred Olson. But I need a golden putter. When I played with Tony Matsumoto, he had the putter to end all putters and he beat me just like that. He gave a ton of money to the school. I want to be ready this time. I've got to step up my game."

Children scurried all around them as the young woman smiled shyly. She was wearing a silky flowered frock. He was in a polo shirt and shorts. His bike was black. His teeth seemed to be broken, or cut off at the ends. Such an unfortunate mouth. She couldn't imagine him kissing the young woman who walked behind as he pushed the bike. But you never knew about these things.

Motoko had told her people at the university just didn't talk about some things. Especially who you slept with. She couldn't come out to her mother and the dean discouraged talking about sexual identity with students. He was afraid of lawsuits.

But here he was with a woman who might be forty years younger.

That morning before class, one of her students told her he was desperate to be an artist. She was fiddling with the computer and he leaned against the podium. "You are an artist," she said.

"But I want to be free to be different," Akio said.

He felt too sensuous to be a man in this country. He wanted to escape from the role of a man. All his classmates from high school worked at famous companies. He was embarrassed to see them again. He couldn't live with his parents. He lived with his grandfather who was spending all this money to send him to university. He wanted to leave Japan, go somewhere he could feel more at ease, more himself. That wasn't what happened here, he said, where everyone thought he should be someone else. He didn't want to end up like his father, a businessman who only seemed to live for his work. He admired an artist who had been fearless. Not afraid to be who she was for so many years. She had wild red hair, she wore purple robes, she painted all her work with big dots. It was a kind of courage he didn't have.

"Nietzsche said, write with blood."

SHARON WHITE

"I know his name but not his writing," Gigi said.

"It made me want to entrust my spirit to the brush," Akio said.

He promised to send Gigi a blog written by a woman whose work he admired. She knew he was talented and she was worried about him, bound up as he was in a country that wanted so much from the men and so little from the women, or at least that's how it seemed sometimes. And wasn't that the same in her country, even though most women told themselves another story about their lives?

She was desperate to be loved when she was young, and isn't that what Akio really wanted? That same longing seemed to have infected her. A desire she thought was hidden for good.

She passed elegant shops with beautiful clothes. Slim women walked in and out of the doors. A man cut in front of her carrying a bento. He held it like a gift outstretched in front of him. Another man in a gray worker's outfit, his hair wrapped in a towel, got into his truck and pulled out something from a paper bag. He had plants growing on a shelf behind his seat, tucked into the window.

She wondered what her husband was doing. She had no idea what time it was at home. He could be sleeping, her little dog pressed against his back. He thought it was such a good idea for her to apply for the position, even if it was so far away, and then when she got it, he wasn't happy at all. He couldn't leave his work. He was in the middle of research for his new book. But didn't she feel great she'd landed the job even if she had to turn it down? He was surprised when she said she was going anyway.

That afternoon she found a note from Richard in her mailbox:

I'm going for a hike tomorrow. Let me know if you'd like to come with me. It's in a beautiful place.

Richard

TWENTY-ONE

She went with him to a small mountain in the folded hills where the trees were almost 300 years old, escapees from the firebombing during the last big war. They took the train out of the city and changed to a smaller train close to the mountain. The first train was packed with people going to work, hanging on the straps above her head. It was a surprise when the tightly packed houses disappeared so close to Tokyo.

She could see small rice fields from the windows of the train.

He told her about rice cultivation. About how in midsummer the farmers start fertilizing their plants. They feed the ears of rice sprouting in the stalks.

She'd walked past shimmering rice fields with Motoko in the foothills. They saw people bent over the plants, their wide hats shading their faces. They were crouching close to the green shoots, she told Richard.

SHARON WHITE

"That's it," he said, "*hogoe*. It's difficult work, sweaty and tiring. You have to feel the rice stalks, see if they're swelling. If the color is right. The farmers say the rice is like a pregnant woman due in autumn. They watch the lilies and hollyhocks to figure out if the time's right. The more attention, the better the rice will taste. They consult the rice."

"And the rice answers?" She asked.

"Sure," he said.

Gardens flourished under clear plastic tarps. Trees in miniature orchards were full of ripening fruit.

She felt guilty her country had destroyed so much of the land around her.

"But it's renewed now, isn't it?" Richard asked.

"Different," she said. The city was so densely built she couldn't imagine breathing with so many people at once. But she did. Like being shut in a spacecraft hurtling through time.

"There's an ancient Shinto shrine in Ise that's been rebuilt hundreds of times," he said.

"The librarian told me about it," Gigi said.

"Jim?" He seemed surprised.

"I don't know his name. We talk about gardens."

"You must have charmed him. He's not usually very friendly."

The path up the mountain started at the tram. Already there were people washing the mud off their boots at a spigot. A girl bought ice cream from a woman leaning out of a doorway. A class of kids wearing yellow caps gathered around the woman. They fished coins out of their pockets for the cones while their teacher chatted with the owner of the shop.

"Do you have kids?" she asked, laughing at the group.

"Two," Richard said.

"Two for me. Two boys."

"A girl and a boy."

He told her his daughter was coming to visit in August. She'd texted him the details the night before. He was relieved she wasn't bringing her boyfriend, a new one who was a consultant at the same company. Someone who was hired to make things more efficient, more profitable. It always meant firing people.

They started up the path. The forest was a replica of those Japanese screens she'd loved so much when she was studying art. *Byobu.* Some screens might have been part of a dowry with a secret message for a young woman about how to behave at court, she'd read. Gigi wondered if the forest had a secret message for her. She touched the needles of the firs. Rubbed some between her fingers, sweet and sharp like lemon.

Richard stepped aside for a line of men coming down the path. "Get it done," they chanted in English, giving Gigi and Richard a thumbs up. They carried heavy packs and climbing ropes.

He told Gigi he knew he didn't appreciate his daughter enough and she felt this. She was smart and honest and very funny. He'd tried to talk her into moving to Japan but she was uneasy about living in Tokyo. Too many people and she didn't want to move somewhere else where she couldn't speak the language and everyone would think she was a foreigner, *gaijin.*

She'd come to visit years ago. They'd been hiking in the mountains when they encountered a long string of older women with broad straw hats maneuvering the wooden boards across a wet patch of trail. He stopped to let them pass, his daughter waiting behind him. *Arrigato, gaijin,* one woman said. Her face was blank and the women around her seemed embarrassed, bowing as they passed him. No one had ever called him *gaijin.* Who knew, though, what had happened to her family during the war. His uncle could have killed her father.

When he told his daughter what the phrase meant she was insulted. Don't worry, he told her, she's just being honest. We are *gaijin*.

The path snaked up wooden steps and then into a cedar grove. She could hear water in a stream far below them. Flashes of light like the gold flecks on the trees in those paintings from so long ago hit her face now and then.

Wild monkeys lived in the forests, he told her. That's something that just blew her mind. Monkeys. Not just at the hot springs, but maybe in a tree just above her head.

Where the trail narrowed there was a tree with a thick rope wound around the bark. White paper folded like lightning bolts hung from the rope.

"It's a sacred space. The tree is holy," Richard said.

"And you believe that?" Gigi asked.

"Why not," Richard said, "the *kami* resides in the tree."

"I'd like to believe that."

She used to think the world's largest city was the last place she wanted to be after her stroke. But that was it, wasn't it? To be in a place where no one knew her and, even though the dean had spilled the beans to everyone, it seemed, she could almost forget about her accident. The accident in her brain. The fissures in her memory.

She said, "The first few minutes I was in the hospital after my stroke there was a nurse, the sweetest nurse in the world. He told me I'd get back everything I'd lost. All those words hidden for now.

"'You'll be as good as new,' he said, 'don't worry, Gigi.' He held my hand during the first night when my family was still finding out the news. My husband was off at a conference in the coldest place in the world, my sons doing something or other. The nurse was my lifeline. He held my hand for hours, it seemed, until my older son arrived.

'Nice mess you've gotten yourself into, Mom,' he said, but he looked so pale, as pale as I'd ever seen him and his hands were shaking as he smoothed my hair. 'You look pretty good,' my younger son said, 'for someone they thought was dead.' My husband arrived hours later. The light was coming through the blinds and I wasn't hooked up to machines anymore."

There was no wind. Everything was still except the water trickling in the shallow stream. Richard pulled his pack off and offered her an apple. She nodded. His hand brushed hers as she took the apple.

"I suppose that was my sacred space."

"You were lucky," he said.

"Very lucky."

She felt relieved when he picked up his pack and tightened the straps. His blue baseball cap was wet.

"We don't want to miss the train," he said, and then started down the path.

TWENTY-TWO

On the way home from her classes one day, she found, by chance, a small shrine tucked into the corner of a lane. It was a surprise there were these crooked lanes in a city that was so big you could drive for hours and still not escape it.

The shrine was reinforced with concrete and covered with wood. Incense was burning. It was in the cool corner of a shady place. She'd read that the deities with the pink caps and pink bibs were in memory of lost children. Jizo.

This Jizo had a stained bib, the same kind she used on her two boys when they were babies. There were fresh flowers and sticks of incense in a little box.

She slipped a coin into the slatted box at the foot of the shrine and picked up the slender stick of incense. She'd lost a baby before her two boys were born, one and then the other not long after the first. It was a surprise to get pregnant so easily when she was not that young, and then it was a loss so great she thought she wouldn't recover as she sat with her husband in the waiting room and the doctor told them that the baby was gone, the slip of child just disappeared on the ultrasound. They were sobbing and the doctor looked away.

Sometimes she thought losing her first child was just part of everything she packed away like those old slippers in the cabinet in the hallway of her apartment here. Fretted and frayed, dirty and lost. Like the time the man, a paleontologist, had thrown her against her bed and pulled off her clothes. It was rough and she'd had so much to drink at her party she couldn't really remember how they got into the bedroom after doing dishes. And he wasn't the one she wanted to sleep with at all, but another man she loved who was at the party too but left early when the fight started. A famous writer and a DJ started the whole thing. She wanted love and ended up with violence. Cops took two of the guests away. And even though everything was sorted out in the end it was a kind of warning that the assault, or whatever it was—was the first clue there was more pain ahead. Her mistake was brushing it all away.

TWENTY-THREE

There were so many days in those months, and then years, after her stroke when she didn't know the answers to the questions her speech therapist asked. She felt stupid for the first time in her life. What was a cup used for? What sound does the bird make? How much is one plus one? Who ties your shoes? Who pours the juice? What time is night?

On the way home from school, she stopped at a florist wedged between a bakery and a girl's school. The door was open and a man with a green apron stood at the counter. His place was full of small pots of tropical plants. He peered at her suspiciously. Delicate jasmine flowered in hanging baskets above his head.

Orchids with white blooms on long stems were crowded together in a box. There were hundreds of pots lining the sidewalk. Near the door were flats of tiny flowers with orange and pink blossoms and herbs just watered. She touched the petals with the tips of her fingers and smelled the herbs. The owner of the shop had taken her money and shrugged when she bought first one small plant and then another as the days went by.

She was looking for a tree to be the focal point of the plants on her balcony. There was a tiny tree wedged in with taller plants near the street. It had a tag with a picture of the most beautiful flower, round deep purple petals and curly yellow anthers in the center. When she brought the plant inside the shop and handed it to the owner he shook his head and got her to understand he was warning her it wouldn't bloom until autumn. By then she'd be back in her other life.

It all seemed so far away. Her husband popping the English muffins in the toaster. Her little dog shaking her toy up and down. The roar of planes and helicopters. A bowl of zinnias on the table. The phone ringing from far away. One of her sons texting her as she drank her coffee sitting on the stool pulled up to the counter. Did she want to go back to that life where she picked up her pills at Rite Aid and brought her clothes to the cleaners? Where she was afraid almost every day?

She walked across the high bridge over the tracks, past the huddled evergreens and across the patio that led to the store where she bought peaches covered in netting. They were soft and large and she cradled them like babies. She rode the escalator down to the store and up to the patio. Where else could she find something like this? She was surprised that the loneliness she felt was pleasant and not terrifying.

Men were trimming the trees around the narrow apartment building. They could be ninjas, she thought, with black scarves tied around their foreheads and huge electric saws held above the line of bushes. In no time at all they had a pile of branches at their feet.

Is this your floor? A man wearing a cowboy hat asked her in English. Yes, she answered, and squeezed out of the tiny elevator with her small tree.

JUNE
Temple of the Heavenly Dragon

TWENTY-FOUR

Three students in her class were always together. Gigi passed the young women laughing in the hall, pushing each other against the walls, tugging on the long lacy sweaters they wore like a uniform. Checking their makeup in the bathroom mirrors. Holding their hands in front of their mouths when they laughed. Her favorite was Chikako.

"What's your name mean?" Gigi asked her while they were waiting for the rest of the students to appear.

"Child of wisdom," she responded.

"But that's such a hard name to live up to isn't it?"

"Hai, Professor." She said and smiled. "But I do well in school, so my parents are very satisfied with me. Not so much with my sister. She wants to be wild. Professor, were you the wild child in your family?"

Gigi laughed. "A little wild. I liked to do things my parents didn't

SHARON WHITE

want me to do."

"Hai," she said. "That is my sister. She has green hair and wants to be an artist."

"And you?" Gigi asked.

"I'm a businesswoman. An entrepreneur," she said with a smile. "Professor, can you tell me some of the things you did to drive your parents crazy?"

"If I tell you, you'll tell your friends, won't you? And then I'll lose your respect."

Chikako giggled. "You are so cool, Professor. It will only make my friends love you more."

She was pleased that someone would think of her as cool. She felt old and damaged, sometimes, and this made her anxious. This was a surprise that she carried around a body that might come across as something very different from the way she saw herself.

She told the students about Smithson's art in her lecture that morning. They could visit his exhibit at the Museum of Contemporary Art for extra credit, she said. She had photos of another of Smithson's projects, Yucatan Mirror Displacements (1-9) from 1969.

She clicked on the PowerPoint with a quote from him: "I'm using a mirror because the mirror in a sense is both the physical mirror and the reflection: the mirror as a concept and abstraction; then the mirror as a fact within the mirror of the concept. So that's a departure from the other kind of contained, scattering idea. But still the bi-polar unity between the two places is kept."

"Professor, I don't understand," her student from India said.

"Smithson works with the idea that things don't last. He took the project apart once he'd photographed it."

"Ephemeral," said her student who wanted to be a lawyer.

"Yes. He placed nine square mirrors in nine places on the Yucatan peninsula in Mexico and then took photographs of them and published them in a journal. The article was titled 'Incidents of Mirror Travel in the Yucatan.' So the mirrors reflected and refracted the surroundings, breaking up the landscape. The mirrors recorded the passage of time, but the photographs suspend it."

"He liked to make things complicated," another student said.

"That's right," she smiled.

She clicked and a slide with one of the photos appeared on the screen. Smithson had hung the mirrors at different levels in a tree with smooth mottled branches. It might be a baobab tree, though she wasn't sure they grew on the Yucatan peninsula. The leaves were green in the mirrors. Stationary, shining. Reflecting leaves where the tree was bare, its roots fanning out from the trunk. In the foreground were decaying leaves. Matted, brown.

TWENTY-FIVE

Gigi's phone dinged. She picked it up from the wobbly table in the living room. A hot breeze kicked up the plastic curtain slats on the sliding glass door. It was midnight at home. And why would any of her family be texting her when it was so late there?

Hi mom!
What are you doing up? she texted back to her younger son.
Woke up. No reason, he texted back. How are you?
Fine. she typed.
Just fine mom?
Great. Really great, she texted and added a heart.
Love you mom, he said, miss you.
Miss you sweetheart. Nite nite
Nite, mom.

It was her sons she thought of when she thought she was dying. She wanted to go back to the time just after the lightning. Just fall back into blackness, but the thought of her sons pulled her across the floor and into the living room where she'd left her phone. Just that thought. Her love for her sons. She didn't want to leave them just yet. Even though they were all grown up and had their own lives. And though she loved her husband dearly, it wasn't the thought of him alone that pulled her back to the living. Not that at all.

And now that she was here in this shimmering place, why did she want to go somewhere with so much pain? The wild boar rummaging in the devastated landscape. But wasn't it important to understand this?

She'd read about a woman who traveled in the late 1800s through the mountains in Japan on a horse. An Englishwoman who complained about the bugs and the noise through the paper walls. Blind men poked their heads into her room and wanted to shampoo her hair. Inside their houses some women wore hardly anything. Dirty channels of water rushed through crowded villages. She was ecstatic, though, about her travels. When she was home in England she couldn't move and spent most of her time in bed. Being somewhere else revived her. At one place she drank plum flower tea and ate a sweet made of beans and sugar. A servant gave her snow in a lacquer bowl. Magical things to transform her from an old woman to something else.

TWENTY-SIX

She knew her life was never going to be a fairy tale. Whose life was? Even those really rich people who everyone raved about weren't that happy, a study told her. You just wanted more, didn't you? And she wanted more all the time. Before she left to fly alone to the ancient country, she wanted the chairs to match on the deck.

"This one's more environmentally friendly," her husband told her one morning when they were drinking tea.

"But it doesn't match," she said.

"Doesn't matter," he said. "When you get those cushions you want, everything will be fine."

"How can you know what I want, really?" she asked. "Sometimes I have the feeling that you'd rather not know. It was easier, maybe, when all I could do was say one or two words."

"Why would that be easier?" He laughed. "I like it that you have strong convictions."

"Do I?" she asked and set her cup of tea on the flat arm of the chair.

There were so many things she thought she'd lost and would never find, and then there they were. At first, she could hardly write at all after the stroke. Her therapist had her fill in worksheets like a child, over and over. She remembered one sheet where she had to cross out the word that was not like the others, like in Sesame Street. Arm Shoe Leg Head. Oak Fir Birch Rice. And all she could answer was two or three of the questions. This is stupid, I'm stupid, she'd say to her therapist, a woman whose marriage was just about to break up, and it would be so hard from now on because she had a toddler and lived out in the woods, and what was she going to do with her little boy when she left her husband. Gigi didn't know anything about this until much later when her hair stylist told her. She was a good friend of Ellen's.

"No," her therapist would say, "you're doing great, Gigi. I know you're smart as a whip. Let's try this exercise now," and she would ask her to finish a sentence with the right word.

In the beginning it was too hard and Gigi would shake her head and say, "That's it, I'm finished."

"When do people eat pancakes, cereal, and eggs?" Ellen asked her.

"I don't know, I really don't know." And she didn't know anything. She thought sometimes all the familiar headlines that used to flash in her head were gone.

She felt as if she couldn't see, couldn't make sense of what she was seeing. Her husband brought out all her art books and took her to the museums in the city. Even when she was an embarrassment, she thought, she went to the lodge in the mountains with her family and listened to the laughter of children in the dining room and watched her sons come racing around the curves of the ski runs. The more she saw, the more she thought maybe there was a person she knew buried under the one she'd become. A woman with a face blank as a piece of paper.

It was astonishing she was giving lectures. Her husband had bought her hundreds of postcards and she'd sit at the table in the kitchen with the sun streaming down on the wood and rearrange the pictures of paintings again and again until she understood what she was seeing. Old friends. A Cezanne she loved. The way he saw trees. It was okay to see trees like that. Not a problem at all. The light, the color.

TWENTY-SEVEN

She saw the old man when she was running along the canal. It was too hot to run. She was afraid she'd have one of her flashing headaches, sparks flying across her eyes. He was walking slowly in the direction of the harbor to the place where you could see the bay as a wedge of water between the monorail and the highway.

At first she thought he was a ghost, but she could see the damp marks on his jacket as she was pumping her legs against the rubber surface of the path. Heavy datura leaned over the track, poisonous, sweet. Someone had told her it was called devil's snare. A white heron, her black legs tucked under her shining body, flew along the water. The ancient man was the only person she'd seen so far that morning. It was even too early for the salarymen holding their slim black briefcases against their thighs. And why was she thinking about her husband, how sometimes he couldn't sleep when she finally could without being afraid that she'd end up in that dark silence, not that it was something she was afraid of when it happened. Not really. Was there something restful about it? She couldn't really remember. A period in a life that had gone on like a very long paragraph with hardly any punctuation. That's what it was like to have her boys. Their lives were the only story that made any sense to her, even though she was doing all sorts of things.

The datura was glittering with dew. The ancient man didn't look at her at all as she passed him. And what if he was actually a ghost? It wouldn't surprise her.

The tall man who played a harmonica, or the other silent man brushing his trousers clean, or the one who was smoking when she saw him on the side of the path. He stood by the walkway to his building. They were alive to her, watching her as she ran past them. Sometimes there were men drinking cans of beer or the large man who watered the lilies each morning outside his apartment. The hose looked heavy and snaked around bushes blooming with tiny purple flowers.

Sometimes her husband accused her of pulling the covers off and he was cold, or snoring and it kept him awake, or tossing and turning. Here she could stay awake all night in the tiny apartment above the canal. The sour smell of the water flowing in from the bay and back out again.

TWENTY-EIGHT

She brushed her hair back from her forehead and walked out of the lobby of her apartment building. The sliding glass door opened automatically. Richard was waiting for her outside.

He started the car as she slid into the front seat.

"You go through a lot of toilet paper," she said.

He smiled. "It's much cheaper to buy things there. And easier to get them home."

"It's really nice of you to bring me along again."

"They have lots of plants."

"A few plants on your balcony might be what you need right now. Even though it's so hot."

"You might be right," he said. He switched lanes and sped up to pass a white van. "Have you been meeting more people?"

"Sure," she said. "And my students are great. We're talking about

SHARON WHITE

Robert Smithson."

"It's a weird time of year here. Summer hires."

"Like me."

"Not quite like you," he said.

"I finally figured out what the noise was in the hall. I thought it was someone vacuuming."

Richard laughed, "The dryer in the men's room."

"Yes!"

"I thought of another garden you need to see in Kyoto. The garden of the Temple of the Heavenly Dragon. There are rocks that are sacred. They're positioned just so in a pond, hidden until you move under the entrance gate and through successive courtyards and into the abbot's quarters where the pond's framed like a painting."

It's now that you hear the central focus of silence, he told her. The pond, like a scroll unrolled from left to right, leads to the presence of the pond garden. This is the moment when you witness the scene making everything else disappear.

"That's what Robert Smithson wanted, too," Gigi said. "A three-dimensional moment. He encouraged travel between the site of his landscape sculpture and the non-site installation. The objects in the museum spoke to the project, in this case Spiral Jetty. I almost stepped on a box in the exhibit of his work at the Museum of Contemporary Art."

"Did the guard haul you away?"

"Almost," she smiled. "But I said I was sorry several times and he waved me into the next exhibit."

She wanted to say more about Smithson but was getting nervous and what she knew was lost between her brain and her mouth. Art as a meditation of transition and change. The kind of entropy Smithson writes about. How he wanted the disorder to lead to transformation. Chaos flying out of the universe. The maps point the way out of the gallery, break apart the structure of the installation.

"A kind of metaphor, then," Richard said, gripping the wheel of the car.

"Yes."

As he swerved around trucks and tiny cars, he was telling her about another garden, one of the most photographed gardens in the world and it wasn't really a garden at all, but a thought. A sacred place to meditate on the teachings of Buddha. Rocks represent the eternal element of nature, he said. The gravel or sand symbolizes the ocean.

"A Zen dry garden. *Karesansui*," he said.

"I remember it," she said. "When I was here a long time ago I saw it."

"You didn't tell me you were here before."

"Ages ago. I do have some secrets."

"With your husband?"

"No, long before that. It's hard to forget the raked sand. So beautiful."

"When a monk rakes the garden he moves the sand like waves. The monk may be thinking of nothing at all."

"So everything's spiritual?" Gigi asked.

They were just about at the big box store.

"I suppose it depends on how you look at the world. It may just be a beautiful garden," he said.

TWENTY-NINE

She found the park by mistake. It was her wedding anniversary, and her husband was thousands of miles away. June twentieth. It was as if he'd disappeared. He'd been away for a week at a conference. It was hard to find the right time to talk.

Mothers watched their children at the sand box and on the swings. They were all wearing black dresses except for one who was wearing gold. Men sat on benches around the park with their lunches beside them. Some were smoking.

She went up to the little hill where there was a monument to someone, but the mosquitoes had already started to bite under the heavy trees. She picked up her bag of books and found a bench that was at the top of the stairs that led off the ridge down to the next street. It was sunny and she was high in the leaves of the trees.

Her mind emptied out, the birds she couldn't name whizzing past her. She'd been reading stories about men who sold their daughters in the late 1800s to women who took them to another country where other men raped them after they paid the madam money. It was a simple path. They thought they were going to the country filled with gold, but instead they landed back home, dressed in beautiful clothes, but no one would look at them.

Sometimes she felt like she'd been sold into another country by her husband, the doctors and nurses and occupational therapists. She was not the same. Not the same at all, even though they insisted she was. You're ninety-nine percent back to who you were, her speech therapist said. But she'd lost so much in that one percent. Years before, she'd won the greatest teacher award and her name was on a stone at the university where she taught. She used to be a brilliant lecturer, have brilliant thoughts and write brilliant books about art. Now sometimes she couldn't put a sentence together when she was tired or felt stressed out. It was hard to concentrate and she could only read for a certain amount of time before her eyes started closing.

Her therapist taught her to recite the sounds of letters over and over until she could read a sentence and understand it. They had a celebration the morning she could read the newspaper.

It was brainwashing to keep repeating the lie that her life was the same as it always was. That's why, she thought, it was so tempting to go so far away where she wasn't expected to know the language or say brilliant things. Her husband was right. The PowerPoints were just what the students expected.

Now she was a blank slate to everyone who met her. She was not competing with who she once was. She should be happy, she told herself, that she was walking past people who had no idea who she was, just that she was foreign, one of the expats who lived in the neighborhood.

THIRTY

"My father was a good friend of Yoko Ono," Motoko told her as they stood in line at the 7-Eleven, their lunch in their hands. A square paper box of salad for Motoko and a plastic cup of yogurt for Gigi.

"No," she said, raising her eyebrows.

"Yes," Motoko said. "Listen, we should go to the village where she lived in the summer. It is not that far and it's in the mountains. I can show you an old road that was the most famous in the prefecture. And a wall of water, hundreds of tiny waterfalls like silk thread. It is melt-water from Mt. Fuji. My father once had a light show there. Purple sparkles glittering on the streams of water glowing in the dark. I never saw the lights. It was long before my birth, but he had pictures of it."

"What was she like?"

"I never asked him," Motoko said. "But I think my mother was jealous. He told her they were just artists hanging out together. I don't think my mother believed him."

If she went to the village where Yoko Ono lived when she was a child, and walked on the famous road, and ate in a dark restaurant on a narrow street, and stood beneath the wall of water would she finally be on the other side of this long slog back to herself? There must be more than the exercises she'd been doing for years to erase those moments on the floor when she had no words.

Motoko told her Yoko wanted to translate birdsong into music. Motoko's father thought that was cool. Very cool. It made him think about his work in a different way, he told Motoko.

G igi looked out at the canal and put the glass of wine down on the smooth table near the fake leather couch. There were lights up and down the canal reflecting in the dark water. She had no idea who lived in the apartment buildings and ate in the restaurants selling beef and squid. On the eleventh floor, Richard might be setting his own glass of wine on his own identical table in his own identical apartment. Somehow, though, she couldn't imagine him drinking wine.

He was at the top of the building. If there was a disaster, he'd have to unfold the metal ladder on the balcony and throw it over the railing and drop down into the canal. He'd told her he wasn't sure if he believed in anything sacred. There were disasters, but just not there at the moment. Weren't they all just over the border from safety, and look at the country they'd left? A large number of people thought chocolate milk came from brown cows. How could he live in such a place? He put up with his apartment. What had been there for so many years. Off and on he thought about buying a house, but the apartment was cheap. He rented it from the university and it was almost anonymous. Someone twenty years ago had furnished it in hipster style.

The fake white leather sofa in two parts. The tiny table and chairs. Like a doll's house. The lamp that was pulled up with masking tape above the rug, so he wouldn't hit his head. The narrow bed and the heavy chest of drawers, the kitchen with the ancient refrigerator and the stove that was hard to cook anything on.

Early in the morning, it was still pleasant along the canal. He told her he liked to walk to the very end of the path, almost to the bay. By the end of summer, the flower boxes along the railing would be spilling over the path. Once a week the man who kept his tools under the first bridge would trim the ends of the tendrils. In a week the deep green vines would be back across the walkway again.

THIRTY-ONE

Workers had covered one of the buildings across the street with blue netting. She could see the billows of a blue tarp under the netting, moving up and down like waves under the net. She hadn't been out on the water for so long.

Once, long before she met her husband, she took a ferry to an island named after the whales that cruised around in the summer. The ferry ride was long and they passed caves where pirates used to hide. Now you could kayak through if you wanted to.

Everything was so much less exciting now. Even though there were still pirates who were brutal and not just the ones who called themselves that. So many countries had been taken over by men with fat guts who thought of themselves as pirates. And people were fine with that. What could she do? She'd rented a car and drove to the most northern golf course on the island. Several men were playing golf in pastel colored pants and straw hats, like sherbet cones.

She passed the sites of Neolithic people who had stone houses with internal chambers and lived by fishing the rich waters around the island. Things hadn't been bountiful, especially when it got cold, but they weren't desperate either, were they? She didn't know for sure.

Somewhere there was a flower that grew nowhere else in the world, but she thought it was too early for it to be blooming. The sun was blazing and her head hurt. There was no way to shade her eyes from this sun, no windbreak or canopy of leaves.

She saw a sign for a café on a hill. It was a low wooden building that looked out at a place where a woman had told her there was a radar station during the last big war. Though she thought, weren't they all at war now, or at least on the brink of a major disaster?

The buildings were dismantled and that's how she felt, dismantled. She'd seen the skeleton of a ram in one of the buildings and the woman told her they hadn't gotten around to collecting it yet.

She bought a glass of wine from the owner who sat behind the bar. It could be the clubhouse, though the building was a few miles away from the golf course. A friend of the bartender apologized for being in a work suit, covered with dust. He was retired, he told her, but he worked a few days at the quarry.

The bartender handed her a crumpled menu for Chinese food. She'd seen a man who she thought was Chinese on the ferry. The cook, she thought, when she entered the other room and placed her order. My wife used to do all the cooking, the owner said, but then it got to be too much.

THIRTY-TWO

Gigi had just gotten home when she heard a knock on her door.

"Up for a walk to the drinking alleys for octopus dumplings?" Richard asked when she opened the door. "It's just five minutes away."

"I know," she said. "I found them the first night I was here. I'm not sure about octopus. They're really smart, aren't they?"

"Smart but delicious," he said. "You have to try it just this once."

"I'm never a good sport," she said.

"Time to start, isn't it?"

"Maybe," she said and pulled her shoes on and grabbed her sweater from the peg.

It was strange they lived so close to each other and seldom crossed paths except at school. They had different schedules. But they looked at the same canal, the same glittering lights at night in the buildings jutting out at odd angles into the sky, and the army of salary workers who spilled from the trains and subways at first light. Someone was always working.

It was comforting to her that he lived above her in the curving tower.

S he was surprised to see Akio, her favorite student, standing at the end of the *yococho* looking into a noodle shop. Red and gold banners hung above the open door. Paper lanterns glowed all along the alley. Inside, people were bent over their bowls. Beer bottles sweating on the wooden tables.

They walked toward him, and when he turned away from the shop she could see he was talking to the person who stood near him. Mike, the student who'd been so difficult at first when she'd just arrived. She couldn't imagine them being friends, but they'd both had a hard time fitting in.

"Shouldn't you two be studying?" Richard asked when they looked up. "Especially you, Mike."

Akio smiled and shook his head.

"Everybody has to eat," Mike said, as Richard and Gigi walked past them.

Gigi told Richard she wanted him to find out how many Italian restaurants there were in the megalopolis so they could figure out how many dishes of boar ragu were sold and how many people were probably eating radioactive wild boar.

"I'm sure," he said, "this is madness. No one would sell the stuff."

"No one?" she asked. "I'm sure I saw a sign that advertised boar from the prefecture with the abandoned towns."

"It wouldn't be allowed. They're very strict about these things."

"But don't men eat all sorts of strange animal parts here to make themselves more potent?" Gigi asked.

"I can't imagine radioactive meat would restore your libido," he said.

She started laughing and almost couldn't stop.

"Really," he said, "it probably would do the opposite. Here's the shop," he said and lifted the red and gold curtain up so they could walk into the tiny room.

.

THIRTY-THREE

She passed a green phone booth almost every day. You could make a call there to someone in this country or internationally. She couldn't remember the last time she'd seen a call box in her country. Country of ignorant men, country of bullies and cars. Country of hate, country of idiots. She wanted to make a celestial call. Every day she thought about her mother. What a strange thing to do. Her mother had been a pain in the neck, really, but still she was her mother and she missed her like she'd miss a hand or a foot or an ear.

In all the stories she'd read there was a path to get what you wanted. And even if you failed, the journey was the story. She wasn't sure what she wanted anymore. For so long it was to talk again, to be part of the conversation.

Even if she opened the door to the phone booth she wouldn't know her mother's number, wherever she was. It was surely unlisted.

She passed a little girl with a pink hat as she walked away from the phone. And then she passed a brown dog with soft pointed ears and bent to pet her. She's six, her owner said. She was the first person Gigi had met on her walks who spoke English.

"She's so cute," Gigi said. She could feel the dog's bones through her shining fur.

She missed her little white dog. The dog she loved above all else sometimes. She knew it was dangerous to love a dog like that. They had such short lives, but she was willing to chance the anguish she knew was coming at some point for the love she felt at that moment.

She passed a woman wearing orange shoes walking two dogs on two leashes. They had bright orange booties. She passed the gray birds quarreling in the trees along the canal and a woman picking ripe berries from a raspberry bush. A basket on the path beside her.

If she picked up the phone and heard her mother's voice, what would she say? There were so many things to tally up as mistakes or losses. But here she was in a country that had lost so much. Whole cities obliterated, wiped clean in the war.

She opened the door and then closed it behind her. She picked up the phone, cool in her hand. It was like picking up a shell and putting it to her ear. She could hear the wind from her mother's voice, she could feel the waves rippling all through her.

THIRTY-FOUR

In class Akio wound himself up like a chrysalis. Gigi was having problems with the slatted shades at the window. She couldn't look at the shimmering blinds. It was so hot everywhere all of a sudden. Deep summer. The heat everyone had warned her about and, then, there it was. The floor of the classroom seemed to shift as she moved her wand on the screen and pointed out the blazing rooster in Chagall's painting.

"He wanted to be wild," she said. "To stay wild, to be untamed."

Akio was there and then he'd disappeared into his hoodie. Zipped up to his forehead. He was usually such a livewire with his spiky black hair and metallic blue nails. But some things were mysterious. He told her he wasn't sleeping. He'd been coming late to class. She missed their talks before the rest of the class appeared.

Akio biked two hours back and forth to the university. He said he wanted to tell stories. His father thought he was wasting his time but his mother understood. He'd shown Gigi some of his work hung on the wall of the art room. Tucked away in a corner. Magical fish with bright wings like Chagall's paintings but glittering with tatters of gold.

He'd worked on a farm for a year raising melons. He said, "I was working eight hours weeding and watering and giving love to the melons. I know now what kind of devotion it takes to grow crops. I love feeling the changing seasons, even the cold rain in the winter."

He felt like some people were born to meet.

THIRTY-FIVE

She went to see the baby owl again. This time she was behind several children who were petting the owl with the back of their hands.

She wanted to touch the owl but didn't think it made sense to push in front of the kids who were in heaven, smoothing the owl's feathers. The owl looked at her the same way she looked at her the first time. Her round black eyes focused right on Gigi's face. The owl was not afraid of anything, just looking into her, not through her as she expected the owl to do.

Why would an owlet be interested in her at all? But the owl seemed to scoop up everything like a child. Gigi wanted to be as expectant as the owl after so many years of just making do after her stroke.

She'd gone with Richard to a mountain. It was very hot, almost 90. They took a bus to the start of the walk through a little village, up many steps. On the bus he pressed his shoulder against hers. The heat from his shoulder against her skin.

She said, "What was it that made you leave your wife, finally?"

"I didn't really leave her," he said. "I just came here and stayed."

"But isn't that leaving?"

"Not really," he said. "She was always open to spending time away from each other. But we couldn't really talk about anything without screaming and throwing things at each other after a certain point. When I was here for two or three years, we made it official. There was a lot of stress. My work had started to feel destructive. I had nightmares for years about working on the neutron bomb. How could I help create something that would blow up people but not buildings?

"Once I started teaching, things were different. Everything had to have a documented conclusion, one that I could trot out for the students. I told them the story of quantum physics wasn't people dreaming up bizarre ideas that only apply in unlikely situations; it was basic curiosity followed through with determination and rigorous logic. When I quit my job and left the country, my wife told everyone I'd gone off the rails. But there wasn't anything she could do about it."

It was ironic that he'd left science and become a yoga teacher just like his wife, he said, something his wife thought was beyond peculiar. He's gone native, she told her friends. Or at least that's what she told him she said. He thought she was happily married again. She didn't have to work. She lived in a house above a river and was writing a memoir.

"She told me I was pitiful," he laughed. "She couldn't understand how I could let my life just slip like this."

"Do you feel cut off, sometimes, from your family?"

"No, just tattered. Parts of me are missing somewhere in boxes. I talked to the Dali Lama once years ago. His Holiness told me he was mortal like everyone else. Uneasy, sad sometimes. You can't shake all that emotion away. I know I'm not a very good Buddhist. But no one I meditate with seems to worry about that. Perfection isn't the point. Sometimes, though, I think about what if I'd done things differently, paid more attention to the kids. Maybe I could have worked things out with my wife if only I'd listened to her. If I went to a therapist or came home when she begged me to do that."

On the steps of the village, merchants were setting out their wares, spinning tops for luck, tofu made from the waters of the holy shrine, books with shining photographs of the seasons. One place had carvings of the Buddha and of snakes and owls. The owls were carved with a smaller owl inside.

Richard took some coins out of his pocket and handed a very old woman the money, pointing to one of the smallest owls. A special kind of present. Two for one.

The woman wrapped the owl in paper and handed it to him. Bowing slightly.

He turned and gave Gigi the package. "Since you told me you liked the owl you saw so much," he said.

What was she supposed to say? Was his gift a sign of anything more than friendship?

She smiled and tucked the owl into her backpack, the small pack heavy on her back. It was a long walk, and they climbed many wooden steps in the forest once they left the little town.

She'd felt so strong when they started but the heat was getting to her and the loud buzz of the cicadas filled the forest. It was a sound that was closer to a giant saw than the drone of the cicadas she was used to at home. The song of the cicadas was so loud it blocked out everything.

"Like frying oil," Richard said. "But louder."

"Much louder," she said.

He seemed like he was thinking about something. She felt stupid that she'd asked him about his wife. She didn't want to stir things up.

The light was flashing through the branches, and she was afraid she was getting one of the strange headaches she had now and then. Exploding colors seeping from the corners of her eyes.

"You don't look so great," Richard said. "Maybe we should take the tram down once we get to the station. It's still a pretty long walk to the top after that."

"Okay," she said, and was glad when they could see the station perched on the side of the hill.

They sat in the front seat on the tram moving slowly down the hill they'd climbed. The sunlight flashed on and off the window as the tram swept by the shimmering trees.

Gigi told Richard her husband looked like a folk musician but was really a scholar. A medieval scholar. He was the expert on *Sir Orfeo*. She didn't expect Richard to know anything about the poem, but you never knew. He was surprising in all sorts of ways. Not at all like her husband who she could predict like a clock.

"And what happens in this poem?" He asked.

"A king, a famous harpist, loses his queen to the fairy world. She falls asleep on a warm spring day at noon under a grafted tree. Not something you were supposed to do then."

"And didn't anyone stop her?" Richard asked.

"I don't think so," she said. "How could they know? She was beautiful and loved, but no one thought to protect her from the otherworld. It was a place where everyone looked human, but was supernatural. They had wants we can't understand. In the otherworld the queen slept under a tree just like the one she loved in our world. Blossoms falling on her face."

Gigi wondered sometimes when she woke in the middle of the night in her small bed if she'd gone to the otherworld and it was empty and that's what haunted her. She'd slipped so easily into nothing after her stroke. Just darkness after the lightning.

"Is there a happy ending?"

The tram was almost to the bottom of the mountain. Richard pulled his pack on.

"Yes. Orfeo was such a good harpist that when he finally went to the otherworld, after years of being a hermit, he was able to charm the fairy king and his attendants with his music and was rewarded with his wife's freedom."

She didn't tell Richard that when she first met her husband, his unfinished dissertation was piled in his bedroom. Four hundred pages printed on the old kind of computer paper with holes along the sides, all linked together.

"Don't you think you should finish that?" She asked him.

"Yes, probably," he said and shrugged.

THIRTY-SIX

She was too fat to buy any pants in the city. Or at least that's what it seemed like. Her mother used to remind her of how skinny she once was. That wasn't really true, but here in the megalopolis, she was always plump. The biggest size was 6 in all the stores. Where did the women who wore normal sizes buy their clothes?

She hated even thinking about this stuff. Wasn't she supposed to be soaking in the magic of east and west, new and old, the past and the present? The possibility of everything being blown to bits or split off into the sea. And why was she feeling sexy again? She was too old. She was married. She wasn't supposed to want anyone else.

She went into a Gap store and picked out several pairs of pants that looked like they'd fit. Before she stepped into the dressing room, the saleswoman motioned that she should take off her shoes and slip on a gauze mask to protect the clothes from her makeup. It didn't

SHARON WHITE

make any difference that she never wore makeup, or hardly at all. When she went into the bathrooms in the train stations there were long rows of counters lit with lights above perfectly cleaned mirrors where women sat putting on their makeup, touching up their lips with plum lipstick.

She kicked off her shoes and stepped into the slippers at the door. The sales clerk handed her the covering for her face and she pulled it over her head. She tried all the pants on, and the waists were still too small. It felt like a strange ritual to step into someone else's slippers and hide her face with gauze.

She took off the mask and studied herself in the dressing room mirror. It was a face she didn't recognize. Her eyes looked brighter. Her skin smooth. She could almost believe she wasn't a woman who'd been struggling for so many years to be well.

Akio told her that the rainy season, the end of May until mid-July, was the second hardest season for the people who lived in the city. Sometimes there were torrents of rain and no sun for days. In April, the time of cherry blossoms, people threw themselves in front of trains in large numbers. Now, too, he said, it was bad if you weren't feeling so great about your life.

"And how are you feeling?" she asked him.

"Not so good," he said. "But I'm making do. I've started a blog about how to follow your heart. How to have self-respect. I'm learning how to follow my heart. My grandfather worked for more than forty years in Tokyo and then he moved back to the village where he grew up. He felt like he was caught in his life."

"Is he happy now?"

"Yes, he plays chess with old friends and grows vegetables."

A Shinkansen had traveled miles with the remains of a care worker caught in the nose. Pictures in the paper showed the bloody stain on the sleek metal. The man had parked his van near the tracks and jumped.

This doesn't happen between stations, the spokesperson said. The driver should have stopped when he knew something strange had happened.

In her own country, people had lots of guns and knives and pills. That was the easier way to go, she thought. But wasn't it all difficult? Even when she could hardly speak, she had a fierce desire to be alive. To be here. The light coming through her pots of flowers on the tiny balcony, the ducks landing on the water below. The reflection of the sun on the towers surrounding her.

Another of her students was struggling, she knew this. And there was really nothing she could do to help her. Julie had moved around from country to country. She had migraines; she didn't seem able to turn her work in. She felt the pressure of being a woman every day. People told her she was pretty, she didn't have to get a law degree. Why was she worrying about anything when she had such pretty legs?

THIRTY-SEVEN

She couldn't remember if she brushed her teeth, so she brushed them again and remembered that she had. She'd decided not to floss.

She'd asked a question, a very simple question, really, at the party earlier and the woman, Terry, had responded with a long answer. Now she understood what a trigger warning was for. The table was small and they were all pushed up against the edge with their chairs. The apartment was two floors below hers.

It was delicious food, something she'd wanted for so long. Platters of flat bread and curries and chopped salad cool on her tongue. The host, an artist who taught at the university, was practicing her cooking skills and had chosen Indian dishes in this improbable place to entertain her guests.

"There were two accidents," Terry said. "The first happened in a dip in the road before the town. You know the place where they filmed that episode?" And Sue, the host, said yes. Before her life in the megalopolis, Terry had lived in a tiny village on an island far out in the ocean. The place where her two hosts had once lived, too. They were transplants from a cold windy place.

Richard was seated at her left and he touched her hand lightly, as if to remind her that he was there.

Gigi turned and looked at Terry who was speaking, it seemed, only to her. The apartment hung above the canal and the sliding glass doors looked out at the jagged silhouettes of the buildings, lit with electric lights.

"I don't remember anything about the first one, but Bill was coming back from town and he saw the accident and the emergency trucks and thought it couldn't be me because I was home, but it was. He held my neck as the medic stabilized my body and they cut me out of the car. The engine was on my feet. It was a Jeep Cherokee without airbags and the steering wheel smashed my face. I could hear the nurses talking in intensive care and they thought I wouldn't last the night. That's why they didn't fly me out to Bergen. It didn't seem worth it. In the morning I was all alone in the room and I found out later they thought I would be dead by then and didn't want me in with anyone else. But I could hear everything they were saying even though I couldn't talk."

Gigi was getting very hot and she took off the light sweater she had on and draped it on the back of her chair. She knew this feeling and was afraid she would panic, residue from the stroke. A flash and then she'd be on the floor and couldn't talk herself. Terry was a doctor. Was that why she felt it was okay to lose herself again when she'd been trying so hard to stay in control?

Terry said, "I thought I was okay to go back to work after six weeks but I wasn't. I wasn't okay for years. I wasn't quite the person I was before the accident. The second one happened less than a year after the first. In almost the same place. Another head on—one car passing on a blind spot and then this time I had airbags. I got out of the car as fast as I could and the other driver was walking toward me on the road and he said, that's alright then, no harm, we're both alive. His car had vanished. There was nothing left but a puff of smoke. I couldn't understand how you could walk away from that, but he did. The thing was, I couldn't feel pain after the first accident, not for several years, so I didn't know my navicular bone was broken and all the bones in my arm until a few days later when everything swelled up."

Gigi stood up. She wasn't sure she could make it to bathroom without falling over, but she did, and she sat down on the toilet and thought about turning on the rushing water sound, but she didn't and then she ran first what she thought was the cold water and it wasn't and then the hot and it was cold and she ran the water on her wrists.

When she got back to the small table with so many people, George, another guest, said, "My wife Jill wasn't the same after her fall. She was taking the dog for a walk and had too much to drink and fell backwards down the stairs and was out cold. There was something very different about her after that."

Richard touched her elbow as she sat down. She liked it that he seemed to be checking on her.

"I knew I had changed," Terry said. "And Bill felt like it too, but that was almost twenty years ago and I feel quite right now."

THIRTY-EIGHT

He only wanted to write about himself, Tim told her, how his brain was on fire. How he couldn't escape the thoughts in his head, like someone hitting on the wall in his room and shaking it minute after minute. He wanted to clear out who he was and become someone else. He'd thought he'd be a filmmaker, but that didn't seem like a good idea. He just didn't get along in groups. He couldn't talk.

The other students hadn't arrived yet and she could hear the dryer in the bathroom outside the classroom going on and off. She fiddled with the computer, praying the PowerPoint would behave and the class would be fine.

"But you're talking to me right now," she said.

"Yes, but it's just you and me," he said.

He wanted to be a screenwriter, he thought, then he could work alone. She didn't want to tell him at that point, the fluorescent bulbs

110   SHARON WHITE

in the classroom humming, shades tilted to cut the blazing light of noon, that everyone had to talk to someone unless you were a hermit, and what chance was there of doing that in this place or this time?

"I'd like to do something like what Robert Smithson does," he said. "So what I make takes place in many different forms."

"Like a story?" she asked. "Different viewpoints but connected by the art?"

"Could I do something like that? Would it be cool?"

"Yes," she said. "It would be really interesting."

He'd grown up in Georgia and then moved to Yokosuka with his family. His father was in the Navy.

Now, outside her window in the apartment, she could hear the starlings chattering on the trees below the balcony. They were familiar to her. At home they flew up in huge flocks when they were disturbed, pecking at wet leaves in the woods. Here they filled the gardens all along the canal. She opened the sliding glass door and stepped out on the balcony.

The woman who she usually saw in the garden was with another woman today. They both wore large straw hats and parked their bicycles. Soon they were bent over the flowers. She remembered those English cottage garden flowers from gardens far away from where she was then. The man who had the workspace under the bridge passed by on his bike. He was peddling slowly and waved to the two women pulling and digging and watering in the garden below her.

The starlings were squeaking and whistling, arguing over the berries that looked like mulberries. She'd read that the last empress of the country had raised silkworms and had her subjects spin silk. The empress also wrote 30,000 poems.

When she told her son, he said, "But Mom, they were very small poems, weren't they? It's not like she was writing epics."

THIRTY-NINE

I just like reading," Clara, one of her students, said after class. Gigi was packing up her notes.

"I don't watch television. I'll be reading and the tea will boil or the dog will want to go out and I just can't put the book down. The phone will ring, I still have a landline, or the doorbell will chime and I just can't put the book down. The house will shake, or I'll have to go to the toilet, and I just won't put the book down. Even when my father died, I couldn't put the book I was reading down."

"I'm sorry about your father," Gigi said.

"It feels like a long time ago. He was sick for a couple of years and then he was gone.

So the book was a distraction. It was about a princess. She'd fled to the mountains with her brave samurai general and a loyal handmaid. Her father had raised her like a boy. She was a real swashbuckler.

SHARON WHITE

Prancing around in the mountains, her gold hidden, her dynasty in ruins. The samurai had offered up his sister, disguised as the princess, on a platter, to save the royal line. It all ended happily. That's what I'm most worried about. Will everyone make it out of the story and get back into their lives?"

Clara was from somewhere in England, somewhere in the north, Gigi thought. She was round like a ball and her head stood on top of her shoulders framed by blond hair. One of the other students, a boy, seemed to be her best friend. He had tattoos down both of his arms and an insignia like an anchor on his neck. They needed the seminar to fulfill their art history requirement for the major, but they weren't really interested in the past.

Her student pulled a flowered kerchief out of her bag and wiped her face. Her friend chuckled. Just like the woman on the train, he said. Not quite, she said, and tucked the piece of cloth back into her cotton tote.

Gigi had watched a mother and daughter share a handkerchief on the train, too. It was something people seemed to do in this country. They had shared hand lotion and then used the cloth to wipe the excess off of their hands. It was such an intimate thing to do. She'd never had that kind of relationship with her mother. Her mother was always the princess and her sister the handmaiden.

The night before, she'd dreamed of her mother, young and beautiful on the arm of her father. They were going to a party. She smelled of the spicy perfume she always wore. Her lips were painted bright red. She wore slim shoes. Her father smelled of aftershave. They were all glitter. Her brother had a tantrum after they left, and she told the babysitter to just ignore him. He'd turn blue and then settle down. He wouldn't choke to death.

FORTY

She was thinking about feeding the deer in the ancient city. She'd done that years ago when she was spending most of her time on the floor with the Japanese poet who lived in the narrow apartment, his tongue on her breasts. Yellow poisonous datura bloomed below the small window.

She still thought Japanese men were really attractive. All that stillness coiled up like a wire. But she knew most men could be brutal, like any men. Even her husband had those flashes of something else. Richard was anything but brutal. He'd become something completely different, he told her, from what he was. She imagined he could just snap his fingers and he would disappear into white mist.

It was their one big trip. She remembered the hazy heat and the deer who came up to her quickly, once she had the packet of thin biscuits in her hand. They were on their way to see the big Buddha. It was

SHARON WHITE

so hot she felt like she couldn't breathe at all, and already this affair had taken away most of her breath and then it was over. Just like that.

She'd seen a woman in the subway that morning rubbing the tiles along the stairs with a cloth. The woman, her head tied in a scarf, dipped the cloth in a bucket of water and washed the wall and then down the sides of the railing into the gutter along the stairs.

Gigi imagined suddenly the water from the bay flooding the tunnels. Flowing down the stairs and onto the tracks where people were lined up waiting for the cars. The music that sounded like birdsong would be playing and the announcer's voice might usher them all into the subway. But everything would be underwater. Submerged.

She knows she's eating too many cookies. She knows someone is always looking at her in the grocery store. The checkout woman helps her count her coins. She knows her narrow apartment building curving above the canal, balconies jutting out, couldn't stand up to a really bad earthquake. It was built too long ago. She knows the white heron nests just under the walk where it crosses the water. She knows she'll never ride a bike in this city, even though Richard told her he's had his bike for twenty years. She knows he has problems with attachment. Doesn't he? She'll be gone and he won't even think of her. She knows it's a miracle she's talking at all. Or not. Her grandfather gave up after his stroke. Her grandmother bullied him. She knows she likes the chair and table on her balcony and the passion vine blooming now with its spiky blooms, like a sea creature. She knows she's not attached to Richard. She'll go home soon. Back to her little white dog and her sons and husband. Here, when someone leaves, it's as if they'd never existed.

FORTY-ONE

Now that it was the rainy season she took the bus to the university sometimes. She could catch it at the train station. She lined up with women bent under their umbrellas and old men who shuffled up the stairs. *Ohayoo gozaimasu*, the driver said and nodded.

"It's good morning," Motoko had told her.

He added something else she couldn't understand. Maybe it was "welcome to my bus" or something like that. She kept forgetting to ask Richard about it. The driver's hands were relaxed on the steering wheel until he was about to start and then he would point in the direction they were going at each turn.

She was tempted on the way home to stop at the noodle shop tucked under the stairs in the station. It was dim and grimy. Kids just out of school still in their uniforms lined up at the counter as the cook

SHARON WHITE

ladled scoop after scoop of noodles and greasy broth into the porcelain bowls. Then she slowly sprinkled green onions on the top. The red banners hanging from the wooden beams of the shop were emblazoned with letters, something her husband would have gotten a kick out of. Such a big sign for such a little shop.

The trucks full of building supplies were rattling across the bridge. It was at least an hour until dawn when the sun would blaze into the bedroom window. Her phone lit up on the small table beside the bed.

Wazzup? she read.

Nothing and everything, she texted back.

Don't go all Zen on me mom.

Ha! What's your father up to?

He told me he's making a wattle fence.

Digging in the garden?

I suppose. He misses you.

So he's digging dirt? Tell him to stay away from the dahlias.

I got a bank account!

Great! No more money under your bed in a sock? Your great grandfather kept his money there. He didn't trust banks.

Sara's happy.

She tried to remember this girlfriend but couldn't for a minute. Dark hair or blonde? That time was so far away. And what was her husband doing making a wattle fence? Something to do with medieval gardens? He'd been elected president of the Medieval Academy of America the year she'd had her stroke. She wondered on and off if he was bitter about all the energy she used up. Was he as tired of her as she was sometimes of him?

I love you mom, her son texted.

And then she could see the bubbly thing that happened when someone was typing. But it disappeared. Did he want to tell her something more important and then decided not to?

Love you bunches honey, she texted. Have fun!

I will!

Her younger son seemed to be the one who worried about her even though he tried to act like a tough guy sometimes. His brother was busy all the time. And her husband was occupied. His months taking care of her had surely taken a bite out of his career, even though he insisted he was just as active.

She put her phone back on the table.

Her husband hated working in the garden. It was her thing. If she begged him he might turn the soil over, but that was it. When she'd spoken with him a few days before, he told her he was experimenting with a thatched roof on the doghouse. Her little dog had never spent time in that tiny doghouse. Her mother-in-law, for some strange reason, had thought they needed one.

"It's a relief, in a way, to have you so far away," her husband had said. "Though I feel a little crazed."

"A relief?"

"Not to be worried so much that you'll have a relapse, and we'll go through the same battle all over again. The fear, the rehab, the struggle. And you're right. It must be a pleasant change to have me off your back. Not breathing down your neck."

She didn't know what to say. She loved him. But at that moment she was very happy to be so far away.

FORTY-TWO

When Gigi walks with Motoko along the river, men are fishing on the bank. Plastic containers of red grapes at their feet. She watches one of the men bend and pick up a grape to thread on his hook. Long ago when she was a little girl visiting her uncle, he used to fish for catfish that way. Near the fishermen, kids toss balls up on the grass. Their mothers sit under parasols, their legs tucked up under their wide skirts.

"How's your mother doing?" she asks Motoko as a blue ball rolls toward her on the grass. She tosses it back to a girl who smiles at her. The mothers tilt their parasols up to look.

"She's happy I take care of her," Motoko says and smiles. "I make her feel important. I bring her honey she loves from the market. I've sort of given up my freedom for her, but what else can I do? She gave me so much when I was growing up."

She could hear her mother's voice as she opened the curtains in the morning or watered her plants on the tiny balcony.

"She's always been a pain in the neck," her mother had told an aide pushing her to the next floor of the facility to get weighed as Gigi walked behind. It was refreshing, she thought, that it didn't matter anymore.

One morning not long after her mother moved to the assisted living place, she had her hair cut and set. Victoria was washing her mother's hair with a dry cap, something Gigi had never seen before, when her mother just checked out. It was as if she'd gone somewhere else and left her body in the chair. Her mother was still breathing but her face was blank. She'd held her mother's hands for several minutes as she sat in her wheelchair. The hairdresser panicked and couldn't stop talking about nothing, really.

Gigi could still feel warmth in her mother's hands, but her eyes were somewhere else, too. How could you leave, just like that, and then take months to die? She was relieved that her mother didn't die while she was holding her hands. She knew it was selfish. She wanted to be miles away, and when it happened she was. Tucked into her bed at home, her husband snoring by her side, her little dog curled tightly at her feet.

JULY
One Hundred Bronze Mirrors

FORTY-THREE

She signed up for an Ikebana course at the university a few days before it started. The art of Japanese flower arranging.

The instructor was a woman who was an Ikebana master. On the first day of class, Gigi bought a kenzan, a spiky metal cushion the size of her palm, and a pink plastic wrapping cover to bring her flowers home. She learned that flowers have a secret life of their own. Their faces have as much personality as a person's. Branches and leaves can show their faces too. Her teacher, Risen, told her that her first arrangement was "alive." She was concentrating hard, watching how Risen positioned each flower and branch in her low plastic bowl.

It was bright in the classroom and the five other women all spoke Japanese, even Cherry from Malaysia. They stood at the long tables and listened as Risen explained how to give the flowers space.

Three hundred years ago arrangements moved in three directions

122   SHARON WHITE

and symbolized heaven and earth and people, Risen said. The common people gained more power then and wanted to decorate their houses. Before that, arrangements were only for the rich and powerful.

Their first arrangement would use three lines: main, additional, and supplemental. Each line is active and shows the movement of the line. Soon Risen wasn't using English at all and Gigi listened with her eyes. Or at least it seemed that way. She just had to watch Risen's hands. The way she cut the stem of each flower and deftly placed it at the angle she wanted in the kenzan.

Her mother had loved flowers and then she didn't love anything. When Gigi was growing up her mother had a long flower bed at the side of their house. A colonial house on a new street where there used to be farms. There was still a farmer who came around in a truck and sold vegetables when they first moved there, and then he was gone. Her mother grew iris that still made Gigi's heart ache when she thought of them, tall, very purple and sweet. There were red roses too. She could almost smell them here in the ancient country where the last roses were blooming along the canal.

Before Thanksgiving, Gigi used to go with her mother to buy mums wholesale from a greenhouse at the edge of their city. It was a place of old warehouses and empty fields. Dried grasses surrounded the greenhouse. Her mother would buy boxes of gold and rust mums. At home she would arrange them in a low bowl on the polished dining room table.

It was funny how the idea that her mother didn't like her at all grew in her heart as Gigi got older. As she sat by her hospital bed those last days Gigi really did feel like her mother had done her best. And what did it matter that her mother's version of love wasn't quite what Gigi would have liked? At least Gigi wasn't happy she was dead. Relieved, perhaps, because her mother was so unhappy. Her mother told her she was thrilled when her own mother died suspiciously one night in her comfortable house on the street in another new development. The cotton bedspread pulled up to her chin, her nurse shaking pills from several bottles into the toilet in the bathroom.

FORTY-FOUR

O hayoo gozaimasu," she said to the 100-year-old man as they passed each other on the path. She thought he would have known the writer Junichiro Tanizaki when he lived in the city all those years ago. He looked like a writer himself, those gaunt cheeks and that dapper hat. And they would have talked about darkness, the dim light in traditional Japanese houses, and how everyone wanted to be like the Americans, and how miso soup was like the darkness, and the glint of gold on lacquer. She was reading a book by Tanizaki about all that. It even had recipes for persimmon and salmon sushi. It took a day to make and then you ate it in the morning for breakfast. He worshiped his second wife Matsuko. She was his muse, he told her, and imagined clipping her toenails, massaging her feet while she was still married to a merchant in Osaka. He left his first wife and child.

Gigi wanted the opposite of obsession. Who could take all

that humiliation?

In those days before she could call up enough words to explain what she wanted, her husband would ask her what was wrong and she just shook her head. She was saying no for yes and I don't know when she knew perfectly well.

It was hard to read even now, several years after her stroke. Something that followed her wherever she was. It marked her, this event. A reminder that she was not quite right.

Even in the city where she hardly knew anyone, everyone seemed to know about her past.

The one-hundred-year-old man would have been here when all the paper houses burned first in the great earthquake and fire and then, years later, during the firebombing. Most of the shining dark houses would have gone up in flames.

No one had told her the countryside could be so beautiful. She had gone on a walk with Motoko who took her out on the Chuo line to a place where there was a very old road. The oldest road in the country.

They got off at one stop and walked for hours until they reached another station where old men were sitting on the benches along the platform in the shade, picking their teeth. Gigi loved the meandering way past acres of fruit trees, green pointed caps on the hard green fruits. The gnarled trees on the terraced fields. She had no idea what the fruit was. She asked a man bent in the orchard, scrolling his thumb on his phone and he told her the name in Japanese and then showed her a picture. The emperor, Motoko told her, had ordered farmers to till the soil here a thousand years ago.

"A persimmon?" Motoko said, "I'm a city girl."

They passed a tomb surrounded by a moat where Princess Yamatototohimomosohime was buried. "Once, Chinese warriors gave her

100 bronze mirrors," Motoko said. "She was skilled at sorcery."

The tomb was too holy for Gigi and Motoko to get a glimpse of, even if they wanted to.

When they were thirsty a vending machine would pop up like a mirage on the next bend. A table appeared where they ate their lunch. A group of tourists just off one of the trains that ran through the valley passed them. The men with white brimmed hats, the women wiping their faces with flowered cloths.

"They won't get far," Motoko said, "look at their flimsy shoes."

Gigi and Motoko had walked miles and still had several to go before they reached the station where they'd take the little train back the way they'd come. The houses in the villages had courtyards of onions strung together in necklaces on the rafters. There was no one in any of the narrow streets. They could have been walking through ghost towns, the orchards cultivated by villagers long dead. Who put the little green caps on the persimmons or the nets on the peaches?

She'd seen persimmons only once before, growing on a tree in California when she was very young. The trees were ripe in November and she had stood in a white dress on the stones underneath the trees, like a priestess. She was reading Greek plays and that was all she had in her head. She was so impractical and knew nothing at all about life and death. She'd left her dog in a house in the valley and there she was in the mountains. Why did days like that come back so easily when words seemed to leave her like old friends, too busy to pay much attention to her anymore?

She wanted to know more about Richard. It wasn't fair, she knew, to be prying. Wasn't she asking too much of Motoko who was generous and open and kind? But she knew, if she asked, Motoko would tell her what she wanted to know.

Richard was a brilliant dancer, cool, unpredictable, electric, but he lived in another world like a ghost, Motoko said her girlfriend told her. Gigi tried to imagine his world, the hut of great emptiness, the mountain streams tumbling. His breath going in and out, in and out.

"How did your girlfriend know him?" Gigi asked. And was that a prick of jealousy she felt as she thought of Richard close to another woman?

"Mai took a class from him," Motoko laughed. "He had a beautiful aura, Mai told me. I only went out with her for a few weeks and then we broke up. My mother decided to move in with me. And you know how happy she'd be about Mai," Motoko smiled.

FORTY-FIVE

It was hard to go a day without her mother appearing in some way. She'd been persistently haunting her for her whole life. A woman who wanted perfection in everyone but herself.

Gigi took the subway to a neighborhood north of where her apartment was in the largest city in the world. The librarian at the university had told her about a museum with a small, perfect garden. She got off at the wrong stop and walked aimlessly past women with composed faces, their gloved hands clutching bags from Prada. Each one was accompanied by her mother. A woman who was an older version of themselves, but just as perfectly dressed in shades of cream, or gray, or delicate floral. She wondered if everything in her life was an echo of her mother and if, since her mother's death, everything was a shadow of that same echo.

She was already hot in the t-shirt and wide pants she'd pulled

SHARON WHITE

on earlier. Her t-shirt felt too tight, a mirror of how she used to feel around her mother, a woman who always wore beautiful shoes.

Her map was at the bottom of her bag and she stopped and pulled it out, smoothing the paper on her purse. A woman appeared at her elbow. She was wearing a navy suit trimmed in white. Her short stylish hair framed her face.

"Are you lost?" She asked and smiled.

"Not quite," Gigi said. "I want to go here," she pointed to the museum on the map.

"I'm going that way. I'll show you," she said. "I'm a guide. What brings you to Tokyo?"

"I'm teaching here for a few months at a university."

They walked quickly along the wide boulevard. "And you're staying in the dormitory?" The woman asked.

"No," Gigi laughed. "I'm near the bay, in an apartment."

"How nice," she said. "But you're very brave to spend the summer in Tokyo."

"The heat?"

"Yes," she said. "The heat, the humidity. It's really quite terrible. Are you alone here?"

"Not really," Gigi said.

"Good. It can be sad to be alone in such a big place. So many are. I was alone for years in one of your big cities. I went away from my mother and father, my younger sister, and the house where my grandparents lived with my parents. It was such a little village. Tourists think they're picturesque. They see the wooden houses with pointed roofs on an island in a sea of rice fields and think how lovely. How exotic. A taste of old Japan, but it can be difficult to live there. It's not the best land for rice farming but the rulers hundreds of years ago forced the people in the villages to grow rice. Wet rice cultivation was foreign to them."

Gigi admired how fluent her guide was.

"Are your parents farmers?" She asked.

"They were for years. They're old now. Most of the people I knew who had any desires left for Tokyo," she said, as they passed a large store window full of bread and pastries.

"I followed a cousin to America. But after I got there I missed my mother so much I thought it would break my heart. I'll leave you here, I'm going to the market. The museum is just there. Look, you can almost see it around the corner."

"Thank you," Gigi said. "It would have been difficult to find."

"Have a wonderful summer. It's my favorite museum. You should really stop at the market after the museum."

Gigi watched as the woman sped across the street, going in the other direction and then invisible in the crowds of smartly dressed women. She felt alone and quite lost for a second, a small woman with dark eyes and light brown hair. She was hardly ever by herself at home. Her little dog was her constant companion. Maybe she should have paid the guide she'd met to lead her down narrow streets into the old parts of the city.

She spent an hour in the museum studying large delicate scrolls with squares of poetry framed by paper, flecked with gold. The light was dim but the scrolls were saturated with color. Her favorite fragment was from the twelfth century. It was deep blue with a poem written by a famous calligrapher. The poem floated on the paper. She was pulled into this otherworld even though she had no idea what the characters splashed with gold were telling her.

In another room there were tea bowls with names, famous tea bowls celebrated for their misshapen beauty. One was a tea bowl from the Edo period, White Satsuma ware, *kintsugi*, broken and then repaired with lacquer from tree sap and gold in the seventeenth century. Gold puddled on the slender lip and then branched into several lines on the bowl. It was much more beautiful, she thought, than it must have been when it was whole.

In the same room there was a case filled with small wooden sculptures. Netsuke, the sign said, Edo period.

"Can you read Japanese?" A young man standing next to her said. For a second he reminded her of the man she loved so long ago.

"No."

"Would you like me to read the description?" She was staring at a tiny pig.

"Sure," she said.

"It's a wild boar carved by Naito Toyomasa and signed by him. He lived from 1773-1856. The netsuke developed from ornaments men hung on cords looped under and over the obi that held their kimonos in place. The netsuke must have a hole for the cord and be smooth so they don't damage the kimono. The carver was free to make whatever he wanted. Many of the netsuke were based on zodiac animals. This netsuke is a wild boar running at full stride with eyes inlaid, pale cow horn, and finely detailed hair."

"That's so neat," Gigi said. "Thank you." The man bowed and moved away toward the tea bowls resting in another case.

She studied the boar. It looked like it was flying, hooves delicately balanced behind and legs curved in front. So the cord that held a man's small lacquer tobacco case, displayed beside the netsuke, could slip through the hole. The boar's mouth was open and he had sharp teeth. His tusk flashed on the side of his mouth. He had a long snout capped at the end by round flat nostrils.

S he stepped from the dim light of the exhibit into the garden where, not long ago, iris were blooming. She could see the hard green pods above the leaves. A walk wound up a little hill and there was Buddha in the garden sitting quietly when everyone else was circling the stream, taking pictures. Buddha sat on the edge of the flowing stream, before it cascaded to the pond where two turtles overlapped on a rock. They were stretching out their green streaked necks, sunning.

It was much cooler in the garden. She wished she'd worn a sweater.

She missed her mother. It was a surprise she felt that way. But grief had followed her. She thought about a photo taken when her mother was about eight. She was at the lake at her aunt's cottage. Her little brother is sitting on a huge cow. Her arm rests on the cow. She's wearing strappy sandals in the grass. She's smiling at a world full of warm sunshine and leafy trees. Her face looks just the same as it did when she was much older.

When Gigi got home, she googled the Japanese zodiac, *juni-shi*. She was surprised to see she was born in the year of the boar. The last animal of the zodiac. One site told her she was brave with inner strength and great honesty. She was short tempered yet hated to have arguments. Affectionate and kind to her family. Another said she was impetuous and determined. Did she live up to what the boar represented? And where did the young man come from who also seemed to love the wild boar?

FORTY-SIX

Gigi dreamed that her mother had to go through the whole ordeal of dying again. She told Gigi that she should go and get the funeral flowers for the house. Her mother would drive home by herself.

"So she wasn't well when she got home?" Gigi asked her younger brother.

"What do you think?" he said. "We've put her in the hospital now, and it doesn't make sense for you to visit her. You've been through all this before."

And she had. The flowers by the bedside, the tissues in her mother's hands, the window looking out at the trees. The empty garden below where the patients who were locked in their building never came out to get some air. Piaf at her feet as she sat for hours watching television. Something her mother used to do constantly and now couldn't care less about. The crumpled napkins on the tray table, the empty cups of water. The straws by the bedside. The lingering smell of the diapers her mother wore that the aides changed and then put in the waste paper basket near the door, until Gigi pulled the bag out of the plastic container and set it outside the door in the hall. The woman who kept forgetting where she lived now paced back and forth in the hallway shifting the bag with her foot. Insisting that her mother's room was her room. Crying in the hallway when no one would believe her, not even the aide who shook her head and turned the woman around.

She knew her mother's body too well after those months taking care of her. She would guide her into the shower, turn the water on and then hose her off with the handheld shower. Her mother's skin was still firm. The pounds she'd accumulated over her life gleaming on her bones. After those months in the facility when she refused to eat, things changed.

How could you live for months without eating anything?

There was so much food in this city. The train stations were full of everything delicious, candies in their own silver boxes, green tea cakes cut into tiny squares. Or noodles in stalls all over the oldest section of the city. A famous noodle maker whacking the dough against a table, smacking the long strings until they separated magically into many strands. Children eating fluted cones of ice cream at the top of hills. Young couples huddled over pastries at the cafés, more French than cafés ever were in Paris. Fat lemons in the market along with jugs of sake and oil.

She was never that interested in food, even before her stroke. But her mother was an accomplished cook. Gigi's husband was the chef in the family and her sons grew up watching him cook. Maybe someday she'd go to a cooking school and be inspired with how to make this or that. But she didn't think so. She was probably too old to take up a new hobby. It was enough to be walking through her neighborhood in the megalopolis on narrow streets or floating past the huge neon signs clinging to every surface when she took the trains.

SHARON WHITE

FORTY-SEVEN

Her neighborhood in Minato ward looked like Tomorrow-land and it was. The monorail zipped above her head as she walked toward the end of the path. The tracks hummed. Office towers leaned toward each other in boxy reflective columns.

She passed the very old man with his heavy satchel. He was dressed as he always was when she saw him, crisply ironed shirt and pleated pants, his dark hat pulled down across his brow. He had hardly any cheeks at all, his face just a memory of what it had once been. He was already a skeleton, but he looked ahead, tapping his cane on the bricks. She could hear an egret coming, croaking loudly. A homeless man with long red hair passed her as she looped back under the bridge. His bike was heavy with plastic bags. He looked down at her and she looked away. Three ravens sat on the rail above the walkway and preened. Were all these visitations telling her about something she should watch out for?

Even though her pillow was perfectly designed and very expensive, sometimes she didn't sleep at all. The trucks banged over the bridge to the harbor all night with a shattering thud. In the morning she'd walk in a kind of pleasant fog onto the red bridge, past the tall trees shimmering in the heat and the tracks and tracks of train lines onto the street where she waited politely with men and women dressed in beautifully tailored suits, past the shop where she bought pots of flowers, up the street with two pastry shops and a noodle bar and a Nissan dealership to the school. Before the school was the canal, dark, just a trickle of water flowing past her.

When she had her stroke it was so dark, like falling into a dark hole, and she only thought how frightening it would be to die, and then she thought of nothing at all, except her sons. She was sure she wasn't dying if she wasn't dead yet. It couldn't have happened. There was her little dog, there was the telephone she held in her left hand. There was the clock and the window and the sun.

On her walk home from school the monster cicadas were singing. It was pleasant to be so far away from herself that she sometimes thought her name must be different from the name her husband called her. Gigi.

FORTY-EIGHT

Was it strange she was dreaming about wild boar? The image of the polished boar in the Nezu museum and the sound of the stranger's voice translating for her in the dim light.

The librarian had told her more about wild boar. How they were native everywhere but Hokkaido and the Ryukyu Islands. How they were fierce and reckless. How they have a long snout and white bristles. The white-mustached pig. Inoshishi. How they persevered with courage and defiance. How they were the one meat you could eat in 675 when the emperor put a ban on meat. How they were loved in the North. How they're a symbol of fertility and prosperity. How fathers in the mountains named their children after the boar so they would be fearless. How tourists loved to eat them.

Could she have the power of the boar to shake off the terrors of the last few years? Was she being stupid about this? It was too magical to be true. But she kept seeing the wooden netsuke carving, smaller than her palm. The polished wood, the tiny hooves, the stiff fur. The boar running. Even when the earth was radioactive and the mushrooms they ate were toxic for humans.

Jim said that you could eat wild boar once a week and you'd be fine, but not every day. At least that's what the government had told the villagers.

"Then why are they killing so many?" She asked.

"Beats me," he said. "They've multiplied three times since 3/11."

FORTY-NINE

Gigi went out to dinner at a soul food place near the university where there were all sorts of international restaurants.

"It's because of the embassies," Richard told her.

People who'd hardly spoken to her the first few weeks she was teaching asked her to join them. Was what she was doing really teaching? After all, she had the PowerPoints her husband made for her to use in the classes. Most of the time she could pretend that nothing had happened. Just like the whole country she was now living in had to pretend the firebombs hadn't happened and two massive nuclear bombs hadn't happened. It wasn't something that people talked about. Motoko told her that her uncle sometimes laughed and said the disaster in Fukushima was absurd. You had to laugh, it was so unbelievable. And it was the same for someone who survived the bombings.

Whole cities hadn't burned to the ground, whole families weren't walking around with skin hanging off their arms, blood trickling down their faces. And what right did she have to think anything at all about someone else's history? Maybe she was just depressed. Depression was a normal reaction to all these things. She was definitely having a hard time, even though the people had been nice. They asked her polite questions and didn't bring up the stroke, and the reggae music was loud and there was too much food.

One of the men had studied fish for his doctorate, why the fish ate what they ate and where they traveled in the Great Lakes of her country to eat what they ate. He knew what kind of fish she'd eaten at a restaurant not long ago wrapped in parchment, bent and twisted with its small dark head still attached. It was a kind of trout, he said, and told her the name. The owner of the restaurant had his baby strapped to his chest and the baby was a very big boy who seemed like he was too old to ride around on his father like that, but all the same, he seemed happy.

She'd been seeing ghosts since she'd gotten there, when she flew out of the sky and landed on the ground in the beautiful country. Not just her mother, but ancient ghosts bent over their walking sticks like the men and women she witnessed in the scrolls hung in every museum she visited. Ancient men and women, some of them wise, with monkeys or dogs. Trudging, moving along a narrow road into the mountains or past men swimming in a river, or women and their children catching fireflies with nets deep in the summer.

Some of the ghosts, the men and almost all of the women she saw, were bent double. How did you walk like that? She never saw anyone like that in her country. And there were flashes of other ghosts. On the way up the elevator to meet her colleagues she glimpsed a woman in a kimono leading a man into a chamber with a beaded curtain and dim lights. On another floor people were drinking cocktails and everyone was dressed in pink.

She wanted to talk to Richard about all this, but he was gone for the weekend. She didn't like it that she felt anything at all for him, but she did. Was it that she was almost a new person in a new life all of a sudden? If she stayed in this city for weeks longer could she exchange her old life and all its attachments for another? After all, that's what he'd done.

When she got into her solitary bed that night she touched her breasts and she was thinking of Richard and not her husband.

FIFTY

In her country, she was supposed to be invisible at her age. That's what the style section told her. Invisible and free to do whatever she wanted.

She was never invisible to her husband or boys or the little white dog who loved her, was she? Maybe they all had ways of behaving to make her think she was important when she was really just another woman past the time when she could shine. But here in the country of rice fields and ancient mountains, everyone saw her even when she wanted to disappear.

The old woman on the train with her blue suitcase spilling open with just picked greens adjusted the zipper on the case, poking the leafy heads back into their prison and looked up once at Gigi, a foreigner on the little local train. A gorgeous boy on the train, who could be a kabuki actor, she was sure of it – and she could see prince after prince falling in love with the slim, graceful boy who, though he was dressed in a salaryman's uniform of black pants and white shirt, couldn't hide how beautiful he was with his jet-black hair and pouting lips – glanced at her again and again as she sat in front of him, his hand lightly touching the strap as the train sped up around the curves and he bent toward her.

In her second Ikebana class, she was concentrating on the beauty of the flowers. They filled the shallow bowls with water, and Risen distributed the leafy branches and carnations and iris to each student. Gigi picked the floral scissors she liked best, heart shaped. They positioned a kenzan in each bowl and watched as Risen demonstrated how to support one stem with another or to bind up a flower for strength.

FIFTY-ONE

She was afraid of falling. She was afraid of falling more than anything else, she was telling Richard as they walked into a restaurant on the fourth floor of a building near the university. His hand was on her elbow. The heat from his fingers. After wanting nothing from this man except a ride to the big store she was thinking about him too much.

His friend, a large man with a cane, led them into the smoky restaurant.

"But that's ridiculous," Richard said, "you have perfect balance. And there's nothing wrong with your mouth. It looks fine."

"What's wrong with her mouth?" His friend asked.

"I had a stroke," she said.

"We all have something don't we," he said, gesturing at the waitress. He pointed to the picture of a bowl filled with rice and something brown. Groups of people filed through the door, workers she might have seen in the morning looking glum and identical. Their jackets were off and they sat down together and started to talk, blowing smoke into the air.

"What about the game," he said to Richard, "you haven't gone completely Zen on me, have you?"

"Not at all," he said. "Did you get seats in the booster section?"

Their voices seemed far away. She'd ordered the picture of spaghetti with peppers but when it came there were tiny mushrooms with dark brown caps and fluted mushrooms that looked like they might be poisonous. The blue hydrangeas were in bloom everywhere she looked. Blue as veins.

Richard's friend tore open the little packet with the wet wipe and dabbed his fingers and then his face, something she hadn't seen anyone do yet.

The wet wipes sat on the counter in the bathroom of her mother's place at the assisted living facility. Her mother stopped wanting showers, and then she stopped wanting sponge baths, and then she stopped wanting anything at all, but Franchesca, the nurse who played music for her mother on her cell phone, always made sure she was comfortable. You could count on her to pay attention to what her mother needed when Gigi was away from the room.

Richard was very close to her at the table. She could smell his clean scent. He didn't seem to sweat. Maybe because he was in such good shape. She was covered with sweat, head to toe, most days. She'd been having hot flashes forever, it seemed, and hadn't thought of taking anything for them and then when she had her stroke it didn't seem like a good idea anymore. Her mother took hormone pills for years. She was nothing like her mother, was she? Richard's friend was poking her arm, "Coffee, Gigi?"

And she said yes, coffee would be great, but she didn't really mean it, she just wanted to show she could be one of the boys, even in this ancient country.

FIFTY-TWO

Why did she want to torment her husband like this? She was thousands of miles away and the weather was unpredictable. An earthquake could happen at any time. She had a yellow safety helmet in her cubicle at the university just in case there was a disaster. Had all the disasters happened to her already? She didn't think so. Just because you'd survived it didn't mean you could float along with nothing at all happening again. Did it mean, though, you could be more matter of fact about the next one?

A friend had lost her husband in the aftermath of an earthquake. Aurora was visiting a place where they were building a beautiful resort on the sea. Her two girls were with her. She and her husband had gone to take a look at the resort. The girls' godfather was part owner. The girls were up in the hills with a friend exploring.

When the tsunami hit, Aurora and her husband had to run for

146   SHARON WHITE

dry land. He spotted the skeleton of a building and led a group of people wearing only their bathing suits to the top floor. The stress was too much for him for him and he died there after saving the others. She had to cover him with someone's flowered wrap and leave him while she searched for her daughters. She thought she'd lost her family to the water.

"I didn't know if they were alive," she told Gigi. "Until I heard from a friend who I met days later that the girls were with another friend, safe and well in another part of the island. It changed everything for me. And then we all went back to the place where Andrew died and brought his body into town."

"Just like that?"

"Yes, what else could I do?" her friend asked.

Her weeks in the sparkling city were lining up into something she couldn't define. Someone was pounding on the floor above her apartment, shaking the ceiling. Some days, there were boxes piled outside the door of the next apartment. She put her students' papers on the coffee table in the living room and sat down on the white couch. It had been so long since she'd read and commented on student work. She felt capable and efficient.

When she and Richard had driven to the big store, they'd taken a road above one of the towns up to the mountains. They left the car and walked to a shrine that was about fifteen minutes away. There was a marker, he told her, that had the dates of the past tsunamis inscribed on the stone. Richard told her he'd been there years ago when he'd first come to the country. He was happy to be in a place so different from his life at home. Now this was home. He'd lived in the megalopolis for so many years.

Yes, he told her, he supposed he knew the language quite well, but would always be a foreigner, like everyone who came here from somewhere else.

Why was she thinking about Richard and the mountains and the prefecture?

It was midterm of the summer semester and she had more papers to read, but she just couldn't concentrate. Maybe that's why Richard seemed so preoccupied. Work? But what work did he have to grade? How could you grade yoga or dance?

She couldn't help thinking he'd dropped out. Like those kids she knew in college who just went off to some farm in Maine and grew strawberries or raised goats. Her parents would never have let her do something so irresponsible.

FIFTY-THREE

She listened carefully as she sat on the plastic chair next to one of her students. Clara fidgeted in her seat. Several of Gigi's colleagues sat behind her in the classroom. It was warm and the lights were buzzing.

Alex, who had lived in Japan for many years, was telling them how the government used building projects to revitalize the countryside. How, when the villages were dying, the government stepped in and built a highway or a museum or lined the creeks with concrete or constructed a dam. The officials thought this would improve the economy.

Alex's solution was villages alive with tourism, but tourism from within. Everyone from the city would flock to the country to taste a special kind of tofu or buy crafts you couldn't buy anywhere else. He was restoring houses all over the place, beautiful 300-year-old houses with heavy beams that might be 600 years old, hewn from trees growing all that long ago.

She wanted to go to one of the hidden villages deep in a valley where there was an ancient rope bridge, but she was only there in the world's largest city until the beginning of August and who knew how long anything would last, especially with the chaos in the world. The weeks were ticking by.

Concrete was the sign the place was modern, Alex said. You could see this all over Japan. He showed them photos of ugly buildings, scars on the countryside. Shuttered houses, rivers bound in walls. He and a friend had made maps of the villages high in the mountains or deep in valleys. A portrait of all the abandoned houses. The red marks on the maps of the villages were where everyone lived. Most of the places had only a few dots, lonely on the map.

Sometimes she imagined herself in a village like that. Cut off from her family, cut off from the woman she once was. The vibrant talker, the snazzy dresser, the woman who used to go out with her husband and entertain everybody at the dinner table with stories.

She knew if she worked hard enough all the words would eventually fall into place, all the pieces of her mind would make new channels in the grooves of her brain, or at least that's what her speech therapist had told her, but sometimes it was all just too much. Shouldn't she, though, feel eternally grateful she was alive and well?

Alex flipped on the lights and the audience clapped. Clara leaned against her and said, "Pretty boring don't you think?"

"Really?" Gigi said.

"Old guy, old fashioned ideas, not even Japanese."

"He's been here forever."

"It doesn't matter," Clara said. "Isn't he an imperialist, gobbling up anything he can get his hands on?"

"I didn't think of it like that," Gigi said. "It seems like a good way to bring those towns back to life."

"It's like that way all over Northumberland. Outsiders buying up all the bloody real estate they can grab. It's daft." Clara picked up her bag and slung it on her shoulder. When they turned around Gigi could see Richard near the door talking to Alex.

"I'm off," Clara said.

Gigi nodded at Richard as she passed them. She felt embarrassed suddenly. When she was outside Richard caught up to her on the steps. "Going back?" He asked.

"Yeah," she said.

"Want some company?"

"Why not?"

It was still broiling, and her clothes felt damp and sticky. Drops slid down her neck between her breasts. They walked one by one on the narrow sidewalk until they were on the wider boulevard that wound past the bakery and the ancient wooden house next to the high school.

"What did you think?"

"Interesting," she said. "My student thought it was imperialistic shit."

Richard laughed. "It is. More patriarchal, maybe. His heart's in the right place."

She was afraid he'd ask if she'd eaten yet and they'd end up at one of the chicken places along the road, but they continued walking past the restaurants over the bridge above the tracks near the narrow cedars lined up against the fence and into the street near their building.

"What are you going to do when the term is over?" He asked.

"I'd like to travel a little. I won't have much time, but I've been thinking I'd like to go to Tohoku."

"That's strange. I've been thinking of taking the train north and then renting a car to check out the wild boar in Tokohu after classes end. Scientists are sending a little robot shaped like a sunfish into the reactors at Daiichi nuclear power plant to figure out how high the radiation levels are now after more than ten years. All of the other probes died."

He was interested in what he could learn from the evacuation zone. You couldn't go anywhere like this except Chernobyl, he told her. And that was in a restricted exclusion zone.

"I'm a boar," she said.

"No, you're anything but a bore."

She started laughing. "No, I was born in the year of the boar."

"What a funny coincidence."

"Yes," she said. "I was really happy when I found out."

"It fits," he said, smiling. "You should come. It's a chance to see more of the country. I'd like to see how the boar have adapted. Something I read said parks and forests are the most radioactive but the boar is thriving."

He said he wanted to see how much had changed since he'd driven to a town near Sendai not long after the accident. There were markers in the mountains above the Pacific that recorded each deadly wave. The last one killed 18,000 people. Men he knew had gone back since the government had lifted the evacuation order.

One was a cartoonist, an artist. Sometimes he grew lettuce to sell. He worked in the crippled power plant. It was good work, steady work, something his friend hadn't had for a long time. One of his jobs was to break down compacted bundles of contaminated overalls and wrap them into smaller packages. He carried a little book the size of a passport, a bank book of sorts, that registered the levels of radiation he'd been exposed to. Once he got over a certain amount, he'd be taken care of for the rest of his life. When his friend wasn't working he played pachinko or drank or slept.

"He told me there are good jobs hunting boar with traps and air guns."

"That's horrifying," she said.

"Haven't you seen the pictures of animals living in deserted houses?" Richard asked.

"Yes. Aren't they afraid of humans?" she asked, laughing.

"Not at all. Feral swine are actually getting to be a major problem in North Dakota and Montana now. They're coming across the border from Canada. They're not afraid of anything. They destroy crops and birds."

"You're kidding."

"No," he said, "My cousin lives in Montana and he's seen pickup trucks full of boar. Hunters love them. They're very clever and survive even the coldest winters, burrowing into snow to make pig-loos. My cousin's part of a group of ranchers that's gotten together to lobby the Canadian government to do something about it."

"That's wild."

"And absurd. They hunt boar from planes with night vision goggles and thermal imaging scopes. They're about 300 pounds."

When they reached their building, he waited for her to step inside but she shook her head. "I'm going to Lawson to pick up a few things," she said.

She was afraid he'd say he'd come along and then she was afraid she'd have to buy something she didn't want and then they'd have to squeeze into the tiny elevator together, and then what would she say if he invited her up for a drink or something?

But he just nodded and said, "Have a good night."

FIFTY-FOUR

Gigi looked the monkey straight in the eye, something she realized later she was not supposed to do. The monkey was sitting on a boulder above them on the trail. She was bending bamboo shoots with her hand, snapping them off and then putting them into her mouth. The monkey's arm was long and furry and she bent her elbow and slipped shoot after shoot into her mouth. Every now and then she'd scratch her rump. Suddenly, the monkey jumped and landed on Gigi's shoulder screeching. One of her students, a squirrely kid who didn't like to talk in class, took his backpack and swung it at the monkey who leapt up into the branches of a shaggy cedar.

She knew it was a bad idea to take the class on a field trip to the monkey park, but it seemed like a way to get out of the classroom and bond. The semester was half over.

They'd talked about different architectural styles on the way. She

SHARON WHITE

pointed out a building that looked like something Le Corbusier would design next to a samurai's house. The train was making her a little carsick and a couple who were speaking French kept talking about how they would soap each other up and then carefully wash each part they were going to suck and put into their mouths. She hoped her students didn't understand French.

The monkey smelled like skunk and pieces of its fur stuck to her shoulder. Everything was damp. She felt dizzy and sat down on the steps cut into the edge of the trail. Suddenly she was seeing sparks and squiggles.

"I don't think she feels well," the student who drank bottle after bottle of water in class said.

"I hope we're not stuck here now," another student said. She could see his feet, but not anything else. The sun came through the trees and then seemed to split up in waves.

"You know she had a stroke," Clara said.

"Shut up," another student said and kicked her with his boot.

"I'll be fine," Gigi said. "I just have to rest for about fifteen minutes and then we can keep on going or turn around for ice cream."

"Ice cream, definitely. It's unbelievably hot here," Akio said.

Julie, who was often missing from class, put her hand on her shoulder and said, "You should drink more water."

She pulled the water bottle out of Gigi's pack, unscrewed the top and gave her the plastic bottle. "You're probably dehydrated. That's what my doctors have told me about these kinds of headaches."

Her face was very close to Gigi's. This steadied her. And the thought that someone who struggled to make it to class at all was taking care of her.

FIFTY-FIVE

The more Richard told her about his past life, the more she thought he'd been spirited away from Earth and sent out to space until the director of the mission called him back, and he landed in the ancient country with the hamlets tucked into the hills and women offering tea on winding narrow roads. Was anything he told her true? The daughter, the wife, the son.

He said he'd been there for ages. A kind of cocoon he'd invented. His wife gone from his life for years, his daughter now in another country, completely different time zones. His son such a gentle kid growing up. Always reading. He loved camping, even when he was so small he could barely talk. When he was on his first long walk, he'd sent Richard letters about green lakes, snow covered passes, Persian deer.

Richard once had a family, a house, even a dog called George who

SHARON WHITE

he fed each morning because the kids would forget and took for walks because the kids were too busy. He read newspapers and drank coffee in the morning. He was masquerading as someone quite normal, even though the calculations he made had to be something quite out of the ordinary. He said the sky was not what it seemed, especially at night. He thought it was very cool that the most sophisticated telescopes made the gravitational field real. The sky you could see at night from some mountaintop on the edge of the city was just an impression of what was actually going on. If they could actually see the ripples in the universe, the sky would be like a lake. Bright, shimmering with dots and streaks and patches of light. Nothing would be static, gravitational waves disrupting the paths of celestial bodies. There wasn't much evidence for the theories he was working on. To prove a new sub particle existed you just had to demonstrate the experiment had elegance, coherence, and inner beauty.

Were they avoiding one another? She wasn't sure. She'd been busy. He was away, she thought. She'd been daydreaming about him. Imagining him doing all sorts of things to her in the narrow hallway of her apartment.

Against the door. He would shut the door quickly behind him and then pull her close and then run his hands on her legs and then up her skirt and then– She never really got past that image. She couldn't do this to her husband. She knew she wanted to be with him in that other life and he was so reasonable he'd say he understood why it happened. Or he'd be furious. How could it not happen? It was predictable but it would ruin everything in their lives. And what was she doing, thinking about Richard like this? There was no way of knowing what he was feeling when he looked at her. Maybe he was just curious.

She wanted mindless pleasure like the days with the poet so long ago. And in the ancient city of Nara when the heat was streaming all through her and the holy deer nudged her arms and back and hands as she fed them one after another of the thin wafers you could buy at the tiny stores where the deer walked in and out like it was their territory, too. Some kind of protection from growing old and sick.

This attraction she felt for Richard was nothing but a mirage, part of the fog around him.

FIFTY-SIX

She was surprised to bump into him by the mailboxes the next day.

"I hear you had some kind of spell on the mountain the other day," he said.

"It was nothing," she said and blushed. "Just a weird kind of headache I get sometimes, when I don't drink enough water."

"You shouldn't look a monkey straight in the eye."

"I learned that."

"I hear Tim saved you."

"Yes, he's very proud of that. They were just as happy to have ice cream instead of going up to the shrine."

She nodded and fished out one piece of paper from her mailbox advertising the yomu yomu club at lunch. She'd tried to learn more Japanese before she left home, but it was too frustrating. Maybe it would help if she went to the club. She knew people brought lots of books in Japanese and read them together. She might even like the anime stories with more illustrations than words.

"I'm going to Electric Town after classes. I thought you might like to come with me. It's a gas."

"A gas?" She laughed.

"Sure," he said.

They took the subway to Akihabara Denki Gai to find new speakers. His were twenty years old. They worked fine for so long, he told her, and now they were garbage.

He found the narrow alley he was looking for and they squeezed past small shops with crates full of switches and cables and plugs. Old men were bent over their pieces of equipment. Customers ran their fingers through the crates, looking for just the right part.

"You can get anything you want, though once I searched for most of a day for a video game my niece had to have or she'd be heartbroken."

She waited for him on the sidewalk, pushed and jostled by people rushing by. Clusters of tourists huddled together peering at their phones. The sides of buildings were flashing with lights. Richard had told her that starlight reached us through a vast celestial vacuum. There was no music, just silence in the void. Sound was, after all, atomic vibrations. Music needed air or water or stone to transform silence.

When he came out of the shop, his new speakers wrapped in paper, a young woman dressed like an anime character handed him a picture of a drink decorated with a frothy design. He smiled and tucked the piece of paper in his pocket as he juggled the wrapped speakers.

"Asuna," he said. "You might get a kick out of going to one of the maid cafés. They're pretty mainstream now. You get to pretend you're someone else. Not the person you usually are with a job and a family."

"Maid café?"

"Young women dressed in maid costumes serve pastries and frothy drinks to the patrons. Some are dressed like anime characters. It's sort of a hoot. The owners have tried to keep the patrons under control to protect the servers. Some have a list of rules."

"I don't know. It doesn't really seem to be up my alley." But she could imagine his lips on her lips suddenly and she turned away.

"Probably not. Just a thought." He laughed.

FIFTY-SEVEN

It was her younger son, her husband told her, who was the one to see her mother-in-law's body, before the police came and took her away. The aide had panicked and called her son.

Her husband was away from the city at a conference and her son was the only one of the family near enough to do any good. Why did everything happen when no one was at home? That's the way it always was. She'd just talked to her mother-in-law and told her she loved her when she really wasn't sure she loved her at all. After all, Grace had been saying nasty things to strangers about Gigi's husband and their sons for years.

Gigi felt sorry for her, an angry woman who'd been angry about one thing or another all her life. The tiles in the kitchen were not really the ones she wanted, Gigi's saint of a husband wasn't really the child she loved but her daughter, the daughter with the beautiful hair

162   SHARON WHITE

and perfect husband who made lots of money. And they had darling children. And it was Gigi's son, the grandchild she was always saying bad things about, who was the one to touch her foot and look into her eyes after she died.

"Now I know what a zombie looks like in real life, Mom," he said when she talked to him. "She was aggressively dead."

"But you're okay?"

"Yeah, I'm okay. It was just weird. I don't think I felt anything. Gloria told me to go into Grandma's bedroom and she shut the door and I was alone. It wasn't her anymore. I did think Grandma did the best she could. Considering who she was."

"Did you tell her that?"

"Not really, not then, but before."

She was afraid that, like everything, there was always some kind of feeling, and that feeling was what got them all into trouble somehow. She was thrilled when she could pull up the words to tell her family how she was feeling after her stroke and then, she didn't want to find them anymore, sometimes, because she wasn't sure she wanted her husband and sons to know the truth, that the way she was feeling was not the way she'd ever felt before.

"I'm so sorry honey," she said.

"I know Mom. When will you be home?"

"Pretty soon," she said. "Put your dad back on the phone, okay?"

There was a minute where the phone was silent and then her husband said, "It was pretty crummy of Gloria to ask him to handle that."

"I agree. How are you?"

"Fine, but strange. It's odd to have that taken off my back."

"I'll be home soon."

"Not soon enough," he said. "But the funeral won't be until fall. Dierdre wants to wait until all her family can come."

"Typical," she said.

"I want you," he said, "to soak up everything you can there. It's not so great here right now."

"Have you forgiven me then for leaving you?"

"As long as you're back in a few weeks."

"Love you," she said.

"Love you, too, darling."

She put her phone down on the low table and looked out at her garden. For that's what it was. Blooming, each color concentrated in its own pot. The passion vine twined around the balcony. The deep blue of the petals. The tree that wouldn't bloom until fall was forming tiny buds. She hoped she'd be lucky enough to see them blooming before she left the city and went home.

FIFTY-EIGHT

She was watching a Korean drama with English subtitles on television. This one was set in Seoul, a city that seemed to have lots of murders and intrigue. Or at least that's what the drama would have you believe. It was about a group of lawyers who got tangled up with a gangster. The beautiful woman, who was the youngest on the team, was the only one to die in the end when everything got much more dangerous. Gigi was sad this character had been killed off. She was devious but naïve at the same time. She didn't really deserve to die, choked to death in a narrow alley.

Gigi was taking care of a neighbor's gerbil and that made her miss her little white dog even more. Her tiny white paws, the way she curled up completely sometimes. Her body, like origami, folded into itself in a knot. The neighbor told her not to worry about the gerbil. He was a desert rat, after all. Didn't need much water, hardly ever ate. What's the animal's name, she texted. Terrance, he replied. It seemed to suit him, she thought. He looked like he wore a little white coat with a tan tie. Give the critter a piece of lettuce or carrot now and then and it will be fine, he texted, and added the poop emoji.

Her neighbor had told her he was depressed. The lack of light sometimes in the summer made it worse. The rainy season and then the heat. He was going home to the UK for a few weeks. "Not much better, is it?" she asked him and he laughed.

"Not really," he said, "but the change of scenery will do me a world of good." He was more depressed, he told her, until he started to take the pills he was on. And now he mostly avoided the darkness. The darkness of his life came before the pills and why shouldn't he be happy? His daughter was skilled and beautiful, like a princess. His wife was a gem. Though he hardly got to see them with this job. He didn't really like being an expat. It was easier to go back and forth. He could do some of the work in his house in the country. That's where they lived most of the summer. And London was so dangerous now with a truck bomb, or fire, at least twice a month. All the terror against one group or another. The government there was just as bad as her country and he pointed west.

She'd figured out in the last few days that she'd fallen into the trap of thinking the ancient country with the beautiful cities and thousands of temples was a salvation of sorts for her. But all the same, she was not as lost as she'd been when she arrived.

She'd gone on a field trip with her class to a place where a thousand dancers in matching yukata, white and black, shimmered at night with the light of 1,000 toro lanterns. It was very dark and they danced together, each one mimicking the next in the dance. She knew she would never see anything like this anywhere else and it made her happy that she was here with her students. Their lives were so difficult. Like her sons were pretty miserable at that age, they needed so much to make them happy.

But now she was here where the light of the lanterns was gold, shimmering on the heads of the women who were dancing. One student who had family living near the place said they'd been making paper lanterns in that city for thousands of years. Once when the emperor couldn't get across the river hidden in the fog, the people who lived there lit his way with flaming torches.

FIFTY-NINE

Kenichi told them he wanted a Jaguar.

"But that's just a Ford," Richard said.

The pub was supposed to be an English pub and it was sort of English-like, with a woman yelling into her cell phone near Gigi, and one by one the bar stools filled with people speaking English but with Scandinavian accents. Kenichi was getting a house. They'd just gotten approval for a mortgage and they'd talked to the builder about what they wanted in the house and found a lot.

"People here," he said, "won't buy a 20-year-old house. It's too costly to upgrade. Not to code, earthquakes and all that. They'd rather have something brand new."

"Like the way they rebuild ancient temples every few years. The whole Shinto idea," Gigi said.

"Yes," Kenichi laughed, and took out a cigarette.

She was having fun all of a sudden, drinking too much and not eating enough.

"My father-in-law couldn't get over the toilets here. He loved them so much he ordered a washlet for his house in Cape Town."

Gigi was afraid of the toilets at train stations in the country, just a porcelain rectangle set into the concrete of the stalls, but she wasn't about to talk about it. She'd turned off the switch on the washlet in her apartment. She didn't need the heated seat or the jets that spewed water or the blow dryer. It was all a little weird. Was it a sign that she wasn't as adventurous as she thought?

Richard said, "The fish and chips are great here."

"Bangers and mash are splendid too," Kenichi said. He excused himself and walked out of the door. They could see him lighting up and then taking a long tug on his cigarette.

"Gigi told me you're going to the evacuation zone in a few weeks," he said when he sat down again. "You're both nuts about wild boar."

"Yes," Richard smiled and took a sip of his beer.

"My brother's lived in Tohoku for years. He had this random idea that he wanted to be a farmer. His farm was one of the few that survived. Most were wiped out all around him. If you go there now you'd see fields all around his barn. Everything else was destroyed. It was as if the farms had never existed. He admired my uncle who lived his whole life as a farmer. He's nothing at all like my father. The rest of the family thought my uncle was nuts. He wants to go back to the land, they all said. Like a hippie. And then my brother decided he wanted to do the same thing. Now it's a mess. He was forced to slaughter his cattle."

The bartender delivered their order, small plates of steaming food. They were crowded together at the table. There was barely enough room to move. Richard's leg was pressed against her thigh. She could feel the heat from his body through his light pants. His hand was very close to her hand as he fiddled with a knife and then put it down.

Three Australians were talking loudly at the table next to them.

They were in one of the most exclusive parts of the city, not far from the university. The bartender wiped the bar slowly with a white towel. Outside, a woman walked by the window cradling a tiny Pomeranian in her arms. The dog swiveled her head and barked. It started to rain. Gigi could see one person after another unfurling their umbrellas with a snap.

"Another round, then?" Kenichi asked and they all nodded.

So you've decided to come to Tohoku?" Richard asked as they walked by the yococho to their apartment building on their way back.

"I think so," she said. "I'm working on this idea about Smithson and destruction and renewal in the landscape."

"And you've become obsessed with wild boar." He laughed and then touched her arm lightly.

"Yes."

That night, she dreamed she went to one of the villages destroyed by the tsunami. She was walking on a dirt road in a place where everything had disappeared except the watery fields strewn with stalks. In the fields were thousands of wild boar. As big as sheds, glowing with radiation. In the dream she felt sorry for the boar. Rooting in the mud, surrounded by fallout.

She couldn't remember why she was there or what she was supposed to do. How could you save these animals? They'd survived the golden walls of water barreling down the alleys of the villages and the junk deposited on the fields. Cars and boats and pieces of houses and shops. She was afraid she'd see bodies, but she didn't. Just the ghosts of those who died, carrying baskets of onions and beets, planting rice in the ruined fields. She was trying to find her way back to a hotel where her family was staying but they'd left already. She knew this somehow. All she had to do was get to higher ground. And she did, running as fast as she could up the steep hill at the edge of the field. When she turned around, she could see the scene disappearing and the boar vanishing. There was only the ocean, deep blue, stretching to the horizon.

When she woke, she picked up her phone and called her youngest son.

SIXTY

She saw flowers in a completely different way since she'd been taking the Ikebana class. That morning, Sensei taught them variations on the three lines. Bending a leaf with a white rim back on itself at the base of the shallow container. Risen adjusted the curve of Gigi's leaf just a bit and the whole composition of sunflowers and pink carnations and two snake plant leaves changed.

In the afternoon she walked past the 100-yen store to the little shed with pots lined up on a ledge. It was the first time she'd found the store open. There were flowers arranged in tight white paper in a bucket on a wooden bench and others on the ground in their own paper bundles. She and a woman with a green apron tied around her waist spoke to each other with their hands.

Gigi pointed to the flowers on the bench and another woman dressed in a slim back skirt and black jacket said in English, "Those

172   SHARON WHITE

flowers are for the Buddha."

She'd been buying flowers wrapped in cellophane in the grocery store for weeks before someone told her she was buying flowers reserved for the Buddha.

"Oh," she said and laughed. "I don't want to take Buddha's flowers."

Everyone smiled and she pointed to the long sprays of pink bells. They were just what she needed. The shopkeeper wrapped ten of the pink flowers in the crisp white paper. Gigi pulled a folded bill out of her pocket and handed it to her. The owner smiled and bowed and then put three coins into her cupped hand.

The other woman picked up a large hanging basket. "Are you a tourist or here for work?" She asked as she walked near Gigi on the sidewalk holding her basket of red geraniums. She seemed so confident, so efficient, balancing the swaying container with her hand. Her heels clicked on the concrete.

"For work," Gigi said, "teaching." And it felt like an accomplishment that she could say that, and it didn't matter if she couldn't find the right word at the right moment, because no one would know the difference.

The woman stopped at the crosswalk and held her free hand in front of her eyes to cut the glare. "The Buddha said, No one saves us, but ourselves. No one can and no one may. We ourselves must walk the path." She smiled and said, "I'm going this way."

Sometimes the miraculous appeared. Sometimes there was no miracle. If her husband hadn't answered his phone when she finally managed to call him after her stroke, there would have been no long pink sprays, or the strange park with the tall trees along a stream not far from her apartment, or the baby frowning at her on her mother's back, or the people marshaling past her in the morning on their way to work.

There was a disaster preparedness festival for foreigners in a few days. Disaster didn't scare her anymore. She was sure she could get to higher ground if anything happened. And if not, she was probably old enough to have lived several lives.

R ichard told her when the tsunami hit, time disappeared for his friend. He was floating in a place where time vanished. The calendar made no sense.

His mother was home grilling fish for his father, his sister feeding the dog. The neighbors were arguing in their backyard. Everyone could see the wall of black, oily water coming at them.

His father's house was high above the city near a marker of the last great wave. His family fled up the path to the shrine and when they came down the hill everything was gone. Smashed, uprooted, torn apart.

Hiroshi turned on the television in the hotel room where he was staying in Kyoto and saw the flashing pictures on the screen. Almost nothing left in some places, the city below his parents' house swept off to sea. How could you believe there was any reasonable order after that? So he floated in that timeless realm for weeks.

He had just come back from a new graveyard where his mother's family was buried. The original graveyard was buried under mud. They cleaned the stone and left flowers and offered prayers for the Obon festival.

"They put chochin lanterns on the grave," Richard said. "Hiroshi told me it was bittersweet to see the flames burning in the paper lanterns calling the ancestors' spirits back home."

AUGUST
Nirvana

SIXTY-ONE

She'd made an appointment with a hair stylist to have a cut and color. She knew it was sheer vanity, but she didn't care. It made her feel younger and not like the woman who went away for all those months, her hair almost as white as snow. She liked feeling different. The golden strands of her hair were a kind of badge that she was on the other side now, even though she really didn't feel that way. She knew there was something missing.

She took a cab from her apartment because the directions were so confusing, but the cabbie had no idea where the place was, so he dropped her off on a street near where it should be.

This is just what her husband and sons were afraid of. She'd be alone in a strange part of the city and not be able to find her way back. How stupid did they think she was? It was raining hard outside and her pants were soaked. Her suede shoes were filled with water.

Gigi walked down the tiled steps of the building and into a hall-way. She took the elevator marked with a three and went to the number of the room from the website of the salon. There was no sign on the door but she rapped quietly and a slim man with a mustache answered. The entry into the room didn't look like a salon. Rows of shoes were lined up on the floor.

"I have an appointment," she said.

"Oh," he said. "I don't think so."

"But I do," she said. "I called a few days ago."

"One minute," he said and disappeared behind a curtain. "You have an appointment now?" He asked again when he reappeared.

"Yes," she said and looked at her watch.

"I think you have the wrong place. This is a recording studio. You don't sing do you?" He laughed. "You want the elevator with the two on the door."

Gigi was embarrassed and backed her way out of the door.

She could see into a tiny room that seemed to stretch the length of the building and for a minute she thought she could see the 100-year-old man bending over his slippers. She could hear the rustle of his clothes as he moved. It was him, she thought, as he turned to look at her. His briefcase was leaning against the wall.

"It's fine," the man said. "An easy mistake to make."

But maybe it wasn't a mistake at all. The building was skinny and the floors were covered with puddles. The hallway arched around past several tiny rooms with blue doors. Would each door open on another scene that had nothing to do with her life? In one, Richard poured water in a glass for a woman who could have been a geisha, in another her husband flew off to another universe in a space capsule. There was a forest full of ancient trees, a pool reflecting on the top of the sky. A long road leading nowhere at all.

By the time she was sitting in the white leather chair at Takumi's salon, he smiled at her like she was the most welcome person in the world. His close-cropped curly hair was dyed platinum. She watched her face framed in the mirror against the white wall. She looked expectant, not familiar. The dazed look she'd had since her stroke seemed to have disappeared. The white walls of the salon reflected like a prism in the mirror. It felt like so much time had passed since she stepped into the salon, but really it was just minutes.

Takumi pulled up hanks of her hair and clipped them with silver clips. He dipped his brush into a little pot and painted each section.

He told her about his village and how he wanted to move back there now that he had a kid, and did she have children, he asked and when she said yes, two, he said, and don't you miss them? A little, she said. The villages have festivals, much bigger than the ones in the city. You need to travel to my village. It is magical. Everyone in the streets holding lanterns at night. Children dressed in costumes, the old women selling sweets and dumplings. It's important for my grandfather to be part of the whole thing. He told me he likes to feel special. He wears the *kamishimo*. That's formal samurai clothes and everyone sees him like that. We are honoring the kami who protect us with the festival.

He was washing her hair. He smoothed her temples and massaged the shampoo into her hair and then grasped her neck with one hand so hard that she almost couldn't breathe, and then suddenly it was over and he was smoothing her forehead with his fingers. So many things she did felt like that. Almost painful but surprising, and then they were over.

"My grandfather calls himself the *ikijibiki*. The festival's living dictionary. He's the elder for the community."

"Have you ever seen a very old man in this building? He carries a briefcase and wears a seersucker suit."

"Where did you see this man?" he asked.

"Behind one of the blue doors."

"Ah," he said and picked up the small black hairdryer hanging on the wall.

He dried her hair and then he said, "Do you mind if I put some product in it? Just to give you more control."

She said, "No, that's fine," but wondered if he thought she was out of control.

He squirted some cream on his hands and rubbed them together, then smoothed the lotion on her hair. And this, he said, holding up several bobby pins. Yes, fine, she answered.

Takumi said, "You have to go to an onsen. Hot springs with bathing pools. It is something you need to do when you're here. It's nice. The women talk. You learn things about each other. You can be just yourself. You won't really understand Japan unless you do. People use it to decompress from city life. Long ago the waters were supposed to have mystical powers. I think they still do. Some are very beautiful in old villages in the north."

Going to an *onsen* was the last thing she wanted to do, even though everyone kept telling her she should. Why would she want to strip off her clothes and step naked into steaming water with Japanese women who knew nothing about her? Nothing at all. She had a hard enough time walking across the room without clothes, even in front of her husband.

She told Richard later and he said, "No one cares about how you look. I'm sure you look just fine. You can wear a towel until you're at the edge of the bath and then set it on the side of the pool."

Maybe he didn't care about how he looked, but she doubted that. He chose his clothes so carefully. Not at all like her husband, who couldn't care less if his shirts were ironed or his jackets frayed.

She loved that about him really, the idea that she had to remind him to buy new clothes. He was, in some ways, the least commercial of men. Was that the right word? He would never sell his soul. Richard seemed much more aware of his image. And he dressed to fit the part of someone who would never work in an office or be the head of a big company. Though she understood from what he'd confessed he used to be quite important. Was he just doing penance for all those years he felt like he'd sold out?

When she told her husband about the whole *onsen* thing, he laughed. "Why do you always feel you have to do everything people tell you to do?"

"I'm not sure," she said. "I think it was my mother always saying I didn't do anything she wanted me to do. I hate feeling like a prude."

"These calls cost a fortune," he said. "But I love to hear your voice."

SIXTY-TWO

She watched the spouting pools as she sat on the bench near
Richard. A cactus as big as a car bloomed in the middle of
a square of clipped grass. Trees arched above men leaning over their
bentos, perched on their own benches, their legs balancing their
lunch. This was the part of the city she liked the least, square buildings
lined up on the streets, though she liked the garden in Hibiya Park. It
was, the plaques said, the first European garden in the country. They'd
walked to the park from the subway.

People were shouting at the corner of the garden. A woman with
a bullhorn and old men in caps gathered together just outside one of
the curved wrought iron gates. They held up banners that said something important she couldn't understand. A reporter was writing in
a small notebook, and his cameraman held the camera pointed at the
woman with the bullhorn. They passed the bullhorn like a bottle of

wine from one person to another. The woman's voice was the loudest. She was the only woman among many men with small backpacks. Her voice rang out across the European garden.

"Do you know what's happening?" Gigi asked as Richard held a rice ball up to his lips with chopsticks. "Sorry," she said, and laughed. He put the rice ball back in the box.

"They're communists celebrating the release of a man who was in prison for years. He was accused of blowing up several people in an act of political violence, fled the country, and came back when the court decided he hadn't murdered anyone, just took care of logistics."

It was her idea to go somewhere different for lunch. He suggested the park. But they were both hungry by the time they got there.

He finished his lunch and packed up the chopsticks in the box. He said he was used to things being pretty calm in Tokyo, really, if you considered all that went on where he used to live. The murders. The car jackings. The beatings and overdoses. The constant blare of sirens.

"I've been thinking of a student missing for three days not long before I left for Japan and then found dead, tied up in a bundle upstate. Her parents put fliers up all over the university after she didn't come home. She was killed by a man she just met in a house behind the athletic center and then carted in pieces to his grandmother's. I was haunted by this for weeks. What kind of world was it when a girl my daughter's age could go into a bar and come out dead hours away in a backwater town?"

"Did you know her?"

"No," he said, but she wasn't sure he was telling the truth. He seemed so upset about this girl.

She wasn't happy she thought more about Richard than she did about her husband. What was she looking for? To be appreciated and listened to instead of wrapped in concern? Even here in the ancient city there was a leash tethering her to home.

Her students helped her forget how lonely she felt, sometimes, away from her husband and sons, though she didn't see her sons very much and she and her husband had been married so long she couldn't remember sometimes what she was like without him, even though he was thousands of miles away. One of her students had panic attacks and another had grown up in Mexico but didn't feel any attachment to the village where her parents still lived. It was so high up in the mountains, she told Gigi, and even though there were monarch butterflies wintering there, it was still no place you'd really want to live.

She was surprised when one student had told her he liked the story of a white tiger he'd read the night before. He was a serious student and knew all the answers to the long multiple-choice questions she asked on each test. She knew he probably had lots of stories to tell and thought it was odd that he picked the story of the tiger. He'd told her his father was an old man. He said he thought he saw the world differently because his father was so old. Old enough to be his great grandfather.

Maybe he brought up the story of the tiger because they'd discussed a stone tiger made by an artist centuries ago. The tiger in the story was the most beautiful beast in the kingdom, but he'd eaten countless men, all the best hunters in the village below the snowy mountain. The son of a hunter who'd disappeared years ago lived with an old woman who promised to teach him how to kill the tiger. After several years, he could accomplish all the tricks she came up with. She wished him luck and handed him a cloth filled with rice balls.

He climbed the last mile to the mountain's peak and saw a speck on the flank of the slope. He shot cleanly and brought the tiger down. But for some reason he wasn't elated. When he got to the tiger, he saw its mouth was open wide and the hunter walked into the tiger's belly following a long tunnel. An old man crouched in the corner. He could just make out his smile in the darkness. The hunter's father embraced him and they stepped out of the tiger's body into the night.

SIXTY-THREE

Gigi told Richard she wanted to do the Super Mario Run Tour in go-karts. Every day, she said, she watched as one, and then as it got warmer, two or three or four tours came racing by on the street she could see from her balcony. Tourists dressed up in costumes. Flags waved on their carts and the characters cheered and yelled as they bumped over the bridge above the canal.

What was wrong with her, she asked him, that she wanted these weird kinds of things all of a sudden? In the trains there was a sign on the back of the seat in front of her to be considerate of the other passengers and not type too loudly. People bowed and said some solemn thing wherever she passed them on the sidewalk or in the corridors or in the supermarket.

Richard told her she could do anything she wanted and yes, he'd go on the tour with her and yes, they could wear the costumes and

184   SHARON WHITE

why not. It was all part of yin-yang, the balance in the universe upended in the country he and she came from. So when they slipped into the seats of their go-karts and started their run through the streets, she told him she felt both stupid and elated.

Richard was shouting at her as she raced ahead of him and the cars were very big and felt dangerous, but she was so happy she was Princess Peach, powerful and sweet, her long pink skirt folded around her. She was in the largest city in the world with a man who was a physicist and then was not and their leader, Mio, a slim woman married to one of her colleagues. They stopped at a corner to talk, and she saw a sign in a window that said in English, wild boar, a delicacy, and the picture of a fierce animal with a bristly hide. Was it the radioactive boar?

They drove the karts around Tokyo Tower glittering with lights at dusk and then along the road past their building on the canal, over the bridge leading to the stark facades of the office buildings and then parking lots full of buses to transport workers to their jobs in the morning. She could smell the bay, a bit rank. It was very dark now and the lights on the bridge to Odaiba lit up the calm water.

Mio had warned them: "Fasten your seat belt, and if you feel yourself rolling, tuck your head and make yourself as small as possible. Keep together. It's not safe to drive faster than everyone else."

Gigi looked across the bridge to where it arched and then flattened on the other side in Odaiba. She could see the huge Ferris wheel, the monorail curving around it. The lights from Tokyo Disneyland blazed on the island. Soon she was far across the span going very fast alone. There were trucks coming at her from the other side. Screeching, honking. She was driving faster and faster along the bridge away from Richard. She knew it was dangerous to be so far ahead of the group.

She felt the puff of air as a car came too close. It was white. Shiny. The kart shook. She put her foot on the break. Was she rolling? She dipped her head and took a deep breath. Her ears were ringing. The thunder of cars and trucks seemed to stop for a minute.

Motoko reached her first. "Are you okay?"

"Fine," she said. "Just a knock. A car came too close passing me."

"Didn't you hear us shouting? And then Mio saw you. What were you doing?"

"Having fun," Gigi said and smiled.

Mio pulled her cart behind Motoko and said, "Any damage?"

"She is good," Motoko said. "Just a small bump on the side of her kart."

Mio frowned. "Don't do that again."

Gigi gave a thumbs up and said, "At least I didn't flip."

"You've found your inner wildness, I think," Richard said. But he didn't look too happy about that.

SIXTY-FOUR

She slit her thumb on the knife that was too sharp for her, actually. She liked her knives dull. There was no danger for her to slip when she was cutting a lemon or a tomato or a cucumber. She got a piece of tissue from the bathroom and held it against the cut until the gushing stopped. Then she wrapped a band aid around her thumb and went outside. She could see an abandoned plastic shoe in the corner of the next balcony. A child's shoe. Dirty rags were in a pile on the concrete. Her neighbors never came outside.

The canal looked soapy this morning. Harbor taxis were pulled up at the dock across from the apartment. Salarymen were walking in single file on the wooden path leading up from the canal to the street. Every now and then a woman, dressed in a black skirt and white blouse, rushed behind the men, her bag held tightly to her side.

Several Toyota Land Cruisers blaring music and packed with men holding megaphones raced across the bridge. Motoko told her they were Japanese nationalists campaigning for the election the following week. They were waving banners demanding an end to the pacifism of Article 9 in the Constitution.

It was oppressive on the balcony. She said the word several times. *Oppressive.* Such a complicated, solid word. But she found she didn't mind the heat at all. Not like everyone said she would. She didn't mind the discomforts of age or the way the blazing sun woke her up in the morning. Her heart was thumping in her chest and she tried not to think of Richard. How she both liked him and didn't like him. He was a comfort in the foreign city. And though she knew he was reluctant to tell her everything, she could tell he'd suffered too.

Though she didn't think of the time when she couldn't speak as suffering, but rather a time when she was inhabiting another body. She just didn't want to go there again. Who would? Her thumb was still bleeding even though she'd held a piece of Kleenex against it for several seconds now. What could you do about anything?

Gigi thought about how she couldn't really comfort her kids after they got to be a certain age. Is that because they were boys?

People told her that girls were even more independent. Sometimes she just wanted to hold her younger boy close and stroke his hair like she did when he was much younger. It seemed like that would make her happy once again.

SIXTY-FIVE

Richard was flirting with the beer girl. She was strapped into a pack and poured the beer from a tube that twisted around from the plastic container on her back.

He leaned against Gigi as the girl passed the foaming plastic cup of beer to him. The beer girl was laughing at what he was saying. Her face was so young and unlined. She couldn't be more than twenty and yet there he was, making her laugh. She had bows in her hair and a baseball shirt and a short skirt on. Fluorescent green like the rice fields Gigi loved. There were four of them at the Swallows game and everyone was laughing, it seemed, except for Gigi.

Sometimes she felt like a left wheel. The Swallows were losing badly 5 to 1. She wanted to just relax and enjoy the game. After the fifth inning, an announcer told them there'd be fireworks.

Bryan, the big guy who seemed to be Richard's closest friend, came back from the beer stalls where the beer was 200 yen cheaper and squeezed along the row to his seat between Motoko and Gigi.

"You're just an old hippie." He yelled over Gigi's head at Richard. "You've been in this country for how long now? And you still haven't achieved enlightenment."

"He's a big deal," Richard had told her. "He has an office of his own and does research on violent monks."

"That's weird," Gigi said.

"Irrational, yes. Some sects condone violence. Bryan's interviewed Gnanasara in Sri Lanka, the leader of Bodu Bala Sena, the Buddhist Power Force, and Wirathu, the face of Buddhist terror, in Myanmar. There's some evidence that crushing bones and burning bodies is a thread in some of the teachings."

Bryan waved a stick of yakitori at Gigi and she shook her head. She'd only been to a few baseball games at home with boyfriends ages ago, but Motoko convinced her it would be fun. Bouncing cheerleaders and everyone waving orange towels for the other team.

"Having fun?" Richard asked her. He could see she wasn't.

She didn't know how to answer that. She was worried about her younger son. She missed her husband. It probably was such a bad idea to be so far away from them even though it had sounded like such a good idea. She was starting to feel more and more anxious.

"Yes," she said. But she was angry he was flirting with the beer girl. It seemed like such a dumb thing to do. Who was he really?

They held tiny plastic umbrellas above their heads and pumped them up and down when the home team scored. They sang the team fight song. His friend drank seven beers and ate several containers of noodles. Richard held a box of dumplings on his lap, balancing the umbrella with one hand, the dumplings with the other.

A group of men with one woman dressed in their business uniforms of black and white squeezed by them. They were carrying plastic bags of food and seemed to call the beer girls over every ten minutes or so to fill their cups.

The woman who was sitting next to Richard was very careful not to spill her beer. She smiled at him and then turned to say something to her colleague beside her.

"What's going on with you and Richard?" Bryan asked.

"Friends, we're friends," she said.

"You know, being married is no obstacle. You're more than a long way from your husband. Why did you leave him to go so far away?"

Motoko tapped him on the head with her tiny umbrella.

Gigi wasn't happy that Bryan, who Richard said was always so wrapped up in his important work, would notice anything was going on at all.

The batter cracked the bat against the ball and their team brought two men in. The woman stood up to cheer and her beer sloshed onto Richard's shoulder.

She said, "So sorry. I am so sorry."

"It's fine," he laughed, pumping his tiny blue umbrella up and down.

The fireworks began and the part of the sky framed by the blazing lights on the field started to explode. White cascades of sparkling light.

She could be anywhere. Fireworks exploding above her head. Summer, the lake, the club, the camp. In her bed when she was really young, too young to stay up late enough to see the fireworks at the stadium. Her little sister not yet born. But she could hear one blast after another as the warm breeze came through the cotton curtains at the window. Her parents were laughing in the living room. Her father was smoking cigarettes and filling the ashtray up to the brim.

On their way to the baseball game Motoko and Gigi had passed the Yasukuni Shrine. Motoko's grandfather was remembered there. He'd died in the Pacific War. It was difficult for Motoko to visit the shrine. Her mother didn't approve. Even the Emperor got in trouble with the press for worshiping there.

Wasn't it better that the dead were the guardians of the living, Motoko said, though she didn't want to put that burden on anyone. She felt there was something holy about those who died. There had to be. And that the dead needed affection, too.

"I would have liked to have met my grandfather," she said. "My grandmother used to tell me I was like him. Deep like a river. I'll send you a link to a copy of a letter he wrote. It's collected with other letters at the shrine commemorating the dead."

When Gigi got home she sat down at her computer and opened her email. She clicked on the link in Motoko's note and read:

October 23, 1944

Can You Write Your Name?

Akiko-chan, you seem to have become such a good child.
Father is so happy for you.
You are playing well with Michiko.
Please listen well to what Grandfather, Grandmother, and Mother say and become an even finer child.
Father is well and has become a soldier, and I am watching you from here.
Your coloring is very good.
Please color more and more and try to draw something by yourself.
Can you write your name?
Is it still too hard to do so?
I will again share with you many good stories.

Please say hello to Michiko and Junko.
Goodbye.
From: Father

She clicked the tab on the website of the shrine under the word
Will and read the last message posted for that month.

As I Enlist in the Army

With the preliminaries aside, as I enlist in the army, I believe
that this joy is not mine alone, but the joy of the entire family. As
I enlist in the army, I deeply impress upon myself the spirit of the
Five Article Imperial Mandate, namely, the Field Service Code,
and I am determined to give my single-minded devotion, despite
my poor abilities, to fulfill my loyalty and patriotism.

It is because of this, as I set out, I am resolved to not return
alive. Even if my remains do not return, I ask that you do not wor-
ry. And during the times when there are no letters from me, please
believe that I am in good spirits and hard at work....

Older Sisters, I ask that you work hard, protect Father and
Mother, raise your children well, and build a cheerful and fine
home that is worthy of a family of an Imperial soldier. This is my
request to you.

At this time of national emergency, for us to be able to return
even a ten-thousandth of the Imperial favor is the highest glory. I
go off in high spirits.

Finally, I pray that beginning with our parents, Older Sisters
and everyone, will certainly live in good health.

Respectfully yours,
Night of March 16, 1944
Satoru

She clicked on June and read:

Last Message

Please forgive Isamu for dying before doing a single deed of filial piety after twenty-two years since being born in this world. At this time I also have no regrets. I was happy to be raised in your warm home. While hurriedly arranging my uniform, it felt as though I was going off to some training, but the seriousness of writing something like my last message brought me a moment of tragic heroism. I pray for your good health. Mother, I particularly ask that you look after yourself. Katsumi, do your best at full speed. Taeko, I pray for your happiness at the marriageable age. Eiko, attend to both your studies and your physical strength, and do your best. Yukio, your words "Older Brother, Older Brother" from the time that you could understand, clings to my mind, and I cannot forget them. When I recall these things, I think of them again and again, and there is no end to these memories.

I am only full of dear memories.

Well then, I go off in high spirits. Please also be in high spirits.

Respectfully yours,

Isamu

SIXTY-SIX

It was just about dawn when the blazing light would flood into the tiny living room from the balcony windows. She opened the doors and stepped out onto the concrete. It was already stifling, but she didn't mind it. A slight breeze came up from the water and already men and a few women were walking along the path below her, headed for the tall buildings across the bridge where the trucks kept her up all night sometimes. She was surprised the trucks booming over the bridge hadn't startled her at all during the night. She'd slept until morning.

She'd taken a ferry once, long before she met her husband. It was an overnight ferry and she had a cabin. Very expensive for the money she had then but she thought she deserved it after years of sleeping in airports on the floor or getting seasick on boats in the lounge. It was the best sleep she'd had in years, she thought. All those years when she was so wired she couldn't sleep a wink. She was twenty-seven but looked younger.

The bed was narrow but comfortable and everything fit into the cabin. The bathroom, the shelves for her things, the little window that looked out at the ocean, the light, the table for her glass of water.

She was going to an island very remote, very empty. Only a few people lived there. It seemed like a good idea. She was all grown up, but not quite sure of who she was, really. Falling in love too easily with men who had nothing to do with how she wanted to be.

When she got to the island after that night of the purest sleep there were no trees. It was cold and the hills were covered with sheep. Some had curved horns. The little bays they called voes were foaming with waves.

She was a volunteer at a wildlife sanctuary. The first day someone brought in a seal they'd found on the beach. A whole family was having a picnic and the seal was just lying on a rock at the edge of the beach. The little boy told her he was sure there was something wrong with this seal. Not more than a baby. The man and his wife who ran the sanctuary took the seal from the back of the car, wrapped in a white towel. Will he be okay, the little boy asked. He's healthy, Paul said. But I'm worried about his eyes. He was dehydrated and birds had pecked at his head and his mouth.

That afternoon she went to a fair at the school. Everyone was invited and she was at a table where she sat with information about the sanctuary. The money they needed. How many animals they'd helped. She'd seen a seal the night before. The seal was swimming not far from where Gigi sat on the rocks, strewn above the sandy beach near the village. Was the seal curious about her? Bobbing up and down almost close enough to touch if Gigi waded out into the waves. The water was so cold you couldn't stand more than fifteen minutes in it and then that would be it.

There was a table of cakes at the fair. Everything you could ever imagine. The cakes had icings that shimmered in the lights, though you really never needed a light in the summer. The sun hardly set at all and this sun that wouldn't go away was both a comfort to Gigi and then not. How could you know what was night and what was day?

If she ate all the cakes would it make her satisfied?

And what right had she to ask for anything, she told herself later. There were women about her age who came from all over the place when there were barrels of herring fished out of the ocean and salted and dried in the harbor right where she lived.

These women lived in little huts in the summer and made a lot of money for their families. They were called gutter lasses and that's what they did. Gutted thousands of fish, their hands wrapped with string, their fingers numb and bloody.

She'd never gutted a fish in her life. But she could feel the frozen blood on her fingers as she looked out across the voe.

SIXTY-SEVEN

What would she do if the 100-year-old man spoke to her? Held out his hand to her. Took a pair of scissors out of his pocket and cut a flower for her. One of the red roses. Gigi would think she'd died and this was the otherworld along the canal. Dank, wet, datura spilling over the banks into the water.

She knew he'd have secrets to tell her but didn't know if she wanted to hear them. His wife was a potter. He lived in the old wooden house with ancient trees wedged between the private school where the children all wore straw hats and blue uniforms, and the apartment building littered with rusted bikes and laundry and bedding draped on balconies.

Sometimes women were beating the futons with sticks.

Today he dipped his head lower as he passed her walking the other way. His shirt was damp and she couldn't see his eyes. Sometimes she

SHARON WHITE

felt like his face was missing. All the same, she considered it a piece of luck that she passed him at all. How many people lived to be that old?

A man she saw almost every day was watering the cannas in front of an office building. He curled the hose around his feet and sprayed the striped leaves. Beads of water shimmered in the heat and then disappeared almost immediately. It was too hot to be walking and she knew it. Soon she might get one of those headaches and then what would happen?

Working with the flowers in the Ikebana class soothed her. It was a kind of meditation. In the fourth class, Cherry handed out two colors of Gerbera daisies, deep pink and white rimmed with red. They used branches with tiny leaves and Solomon's seal with its white and green gently drooping leaves.

SIXTY-EIGHT

Gigi poured more iced tea from the plastic pitcher on the table into their cups. They were sitting outside, almost on the busy road where buses came by every few minutes and she could smell the river, a trickle in its concrete bed below the highway. They were ten minutes away from the university. The semester was almost over. She'd taught her last class in the morning. She could hear Richard's friend Bryan yelling at a student in the faculty room. He told her, although she had a doctor's letter that said she could miss as many classes as she wanted, it wouldn't work in his anthropology class. Anxiety was no excuse.

She'd miss her students and the rush she felt standing in front of the class. She was worried about Akio. He told her everyone around him wanted him to stand up like a grownup. "But I don't have any vision of the kind of adult I wish to be," he said.

Two young women pushed by their table and opened the door of the air-conditioned restaurant. They smelled of perfume and cigarettes. "French tourists," Motoko said. "It's that time of year when they all arrive."

A truck blasted by puffing diesel.

Motoko said, "I've been thinking about my father. I don't know why. Whatever. But I took a trip with him before he died."

"I'm sorry," Gigi said, "when did he die?"

"Quite a while ago. After some years of making my mother crazy he finally decided he'd had enough. I kind of understood who he was though a little better after this trip. He loved Kawabata. He was his favorite author. And Snow Country was his favorite book. We took a special train to the village where Kawabata wrote the book. When we came out of the tunnel and saw the mountains, my father said, look it's just like he says in the book. And it was. The village opened out before us and my father started gathering our things in the train.

"He'd worn a hat, a very big black hat that he pulled down across his face like a gangster in one of those old movies, and picked up his bag. It was one of the first years I was teaching here and I was happy to be out of Tokyo. We never spent much time together on our own. Usually my mother was always with us. He could be very funny, very charming if he wanted to be. Especially if he was doing something he wanted to do. We were staying at the onsen where Kawabata wrote Snow Country.

"We walked from the train to the hotel. My father insisted we should get a feel for the town and I didn't want to argue with him, he seemed so happy. I had a little backpack with my things. And I knew if he got too tired I would have to pick up his bag and carry it. Though I also knew he would never let me help him with anything.

"I followed him up the steep road to the onsen and there was a bus at the entrance. My father wasn't happy about this, but I told him to laugh it off. We were tourists, too, weren't we? Not like them, he said, not anything like them and we both laughed. We left our bags with the clerk at the desk because my father wanted, before we checked in, to see the place where Kawabata spent those months writing the book. There was an escalator up to the second floor. The hotel was very dark. At the top of the escalator was a room with photos of Kawabata and the girl who inspired his book. A beautiful girl with a heart shaped face and deep eyes. My father stopped at each photo and ran his fingers over the frames. I was happy no one was there to see him do this. There were pictures of snow piled up to the eaves and the onsen was a dark wood building then. Now it was covered with concrete. It was perfectly quiet on the second floor. I wondered where all the people were who had come off the bus.

"There were stones on the floor leading into the rooms where Kawabata slept and wrote. He had the whole corner of the original building. It was like his own house. The polished wood, the tatami mats, the bowls of tea, the shoji doors, the silky pillows, the alcoves with flowers. He wrote looking out at the mountains and we could stand there and imagine we were with him above the pointed trees and the green hills that went on forever. Below us was a little log house that was probably there when Kawabata was writing in the room. He came back when they made a movie of the book and, in the photos, the girl was much older and looked nothing like she looked when she was young and beautiful. He was dressed like a rich old man and the town was still filled with snow, but soon, not that long after, it would be much bigger and full of tourists. My father and I stood for a long time looking out at the view. I knew he was very moved by being so close to Kawabata."

A group of men, their hair slicked back or sticking straight up from their foreheads jostled against Gigi's chair. "Cool guys," Motoko said. "They make so much money they don't know what to do with it."

"Oh, look," Motoko said, "everyone is leaving. We're almost out of time too, aren't we?"

Gigi looked at her watch and nodded.

As they got up to leave, Motoko said, "He killed himself," and for a minute Gigi was afraid Motoko meant her father. She must have looked surprised because Motoko laughed and said, "No, not my father. Kawabata killed himself. My father died when he was very old, quite a bit older than my mother. My father just went to sleep one night and didn't wake up."

SIXTY-NINE

She was on the subway going to the farmers market where she could get Meyer lemons and fresh bread and honey. It was late morning and the car was still full of people. She glanced at her reflection in the window and was surprised to see her face and not her mother's. Since her mother's death she'd been imagining her popping up in places like the grocery store, telling Gigi she'd picked the wrong mayonnaise.

Her mother's oval face and arched eyebrows, her mother's half smile. Her mother's smooth hair. Instead, Gigi saw her hair wild from the humidity, her round shoulders, the different shape of her face. A little off kilter, she thought, since her stroke.

She wanted to ask Akio, who commuted two hours there and back on his bike, if he had one of the little motors that powered the mothers up and down hills in the city. A child on the front and one

204   SHARON WHITE

on the back. She felt terrorized by them some mornings on her way to school. The mothers' eyes glazed. And later, the children tucked away in their classrooms, the mothers off to a day by themselves. They careened this way and that on the sidewalks, ferocious and out of control. She was sure she'd be hit at some point.

She wondered where the man who she knew so well for so few days such a long time ago was. That's how you got yourself in trouble. Wanting the taste of something you had when you were young. Wanting the taste of his lips on her lips when that was all there was, really, to the days in the tiny apartment. The sweet datura heavy outside the window, the heron flying past. Maybe driving north with Richard to the prefecture that was out of bounds not that long ago was equally stupid. Maybe spending so much time with Richard wasn't such a good idea.

She thought about her husband. The way he brought her tea in bed in the morning and decided to iron all the napkins one day when they'd been using wrinkled napkins for years.

SEVENTY

Gigi dreamed Richard had a gun. In the dream she was invisible, a ghost, watching him. He pulled open the thin wooden door of the cupboard and searched in the back. She knew hidden in the cupboard by the door were thirty slippers. Just like in her apartment. They were lined up like soldiers, their dirty soles and frayed edges. When he found the gun, a beautiful gun with a wooden handle engraved with kanji, he unwrapped it from an old undershirt and then put it on the low coffee table in the living room. It was still dark and the plastic sheeting on the building across the canal slapped in the wind. He called someone on his cell phone. I'll kill myself if you don't tell me you love me. It was raining. The rain on the windows made a drumming sound in the dream and the patter got louder and louder. He took the gun in his hand, opened the door to the balcony and stepped out on the concrete. He took deep breaths and then threw

SHARON WHITE

the gun into the canal eleven floors below. It hit the water cleanly like a diver.

The dream was so real she wondered if he did have a gun hidden somewhere in his apartment.

SEVENTY-ONE

Richard was very close to her in the elevator at the university. She had on bright orange sneakers and he kicked one playfully. "So," he said, "how does it look for our trip to Tohoku? Have you graded all your essays?"

"Barely," she said, "but I should have time."

"We can take an early shinkansen to Sendai and then rent a car to drive to Hiroshi's village. I'd like to see what the radiation is in one of the villages on the way. Let's stay at a hotel not far from the nearest city in the exclusion zone."

She was excited but didn't want to show him she was excited. After all, she'd spent so many nights alone, sitting on the narrow balcony looking at the lights on the water and smelling the sour rush of the salt water. Those hours just after her stroke came back to her when she couldn't sleep. The lightning and then the pain and the way every-

208   SHARON WHITE

thing was spinning when she opened her eyes. She was caught inside her brain. It was dark, so dark there.

"That sounds fine."

"Any interest in lunch?"

"Sure," she said.

"Let's splurge and buy lunch at the shop around the corner."

"I had a scary dream last night about you."

"Really?"

"I don't remember much except that you had a gun."

"Not like me to have a gun."

"You threw it away off the balcony into the water."

'Good idea," he said.

They walked down the steps in front of the university's only building and passed two students leaning toward each other on the sidewalk. They were dressed in almost identical outfits. Like twins. It was so hot out Gigi could barely breathe.

At the shop the woman who sold the food was always so kind, but secretly Gigi thought she didn't like her at all. She was much nicer to people who weren't foreigners, lavishing them with conversation and bows. Motoko said it's a discreet way of letting someone know how you feel. In Kyoto, if your host offers tea at the end of the meal, it's a sign that you should leave. The party's over.

Sometimes she felt like she was on display and other times she thought she could live in the city forever and ever. In the country she'd become used to the kindness of strangers, women chasing after her with cups of tea or handfuls of ripe fruit. Motoko took her on trips to the coast where they walked along the water and then ate ice cream under tall cedars. They found memorials in the woods of ancient battles and a track that crumbled under their feet as the waves crashed against the black rocks below them. Attendants at the little train stations pointed them in the right direction and waved as they boarded the trains.

SEVENTY-TWO

Motoko turned as Gigi walked behind her desk. "Are you going anywhere this weekend?"

"I think so." She wasn't sure she wanted to say more. Was there some kind of unspoken rule about going away overnight with a male colleague?

"I might go with Richard on a trip to Tohoku."

Motoko picked up the stuffed giraffe on her desk and wiggled the animal near Gigi.

"Have you told your husband about Richard? I know he seems safe but you never know about men."

Gigi laughed, "I think he's more than safe."

"But you must confess," Motoko smiled, "that you're attracted to him."

"Maybe," Gigi said.

"And he, obviously, would be all over you if you weren't married."

She used to be so good at lying before her stroke. She kept all sorts of secrets for years. Those days with the man she thought she loved in Tokyo, cravings no one knew about, how she really felt about most things. It was easier to be cheerful. Now it seemed like it was easier to tell the truth. Not to struggle to hide her feelings. It was still so easy after several years to get tired. Tired of searching for words, tired of keeping up with the conversation, tired of knowing she'd missed the first few phrases of what her students were saying to her. She was a beat behind them.

Motoko frowned and said, "My uncle lived in a town not far from the reactor meltdown in Fukushima. He's a dairy farmer. At first they told him he could stay. The cows' milk was fine. He could still sell it. There was a calf by her mother even though the mother was dead. She was the only animal alive in the stalls of the farm up the hill. A little calf with big brown eyes, so gentle. My uncle rescued her, but for what? They were all killed in the end. The government lied, and two weeks later he was loading his cows onto a truck that took them to the slaughter house and now, according to the government, all his milk was contaminated."

Gigi picked up a pile of tests from her desk and put them into her bag. "I saw a film once about Jamaica. How the farmers there had to empty their milk tanks when the price got too low. It just wasn't worth it to transport the milk. All that work going down the drain. How's your uncle now?"

Motoko swiveled her chair around and looked out the window, the sun blazing through the blinds.

"Not good. All these years later, he still doesn't know the truth. His home is empty and other people from the town are living in temporary housing. He left his dog, a sweet smart dog, and then they wouldn't let him back into the town and he knew his dog must have died on that leash. No one to feed her, no one to bring her water, no one to set her free. When he went back months later with my aunt to collect what they could, the rope was cut, so he hoped someone had let the dog go and she was fine."

She fiddled with her hair, streaked with pink now. "It may not be such a good idea to drive north. There are more interesting places to go to. We haven't been to Nikko yet."

Gigi felt embarrassed. It's not like the prefecture was open for sightseeing now. But the more she learned about the disaster the more she thought it was important to understand that kind of loss.

"It must have been horrible," she said.

"You probably saw all those pictures of the big black wave and the hundreds of cars floating in the water. My uncle was lucky. His village was above the high-water mark even though it was too close to the nuclear power plant to be safe. When my aunt went back to their house and saw what had happened to her garden, she was so upset my uncle thought she'd hurt herself. But he reminded her of her children who have lives in Tokyo and would be lost if their mother died there in her garden. She still has a hard time. The last time I saw her she couldn't stop crying. It's not safe."

"That's terrible," Gigi said and sat down in her cubicle. "I was thinking it's important to see what happened. To understand what people lost." And the minute she said this she knew it didn't make sense. What she had lost was nothing compared to what thousands of people had lost in Tohoku.

Motoko leaned over the partition between their desks. "You know even if someone wasn't affected by the disasters, they still had to deal with the whole idea of being survivors. They felt like the hibakusha after Hiroshima and Nagasaki. Doomed ones. Somehow contagious. Some of the places looked perfectly fine, but they weren't. Even if just one person in the community lost someone, the village was not fine. It was like there were ripples from her loss to everyone around. It was heartbreaking to have to kill your animals. Not just because the cattle were sometimes worth 5,000 yen each, but the loss of the tradition. It was the farmer's life. They were part of his family."

SEVENTY-THREE

She was cleaning out the closet in the tiny hallway of her apartment after lunch. She only had less than two weeks before she took the train to Narita to catch her plane home. She started sorting papers squirreled away by summer hires from years before.

Tractor-feed paper from old printers, lots of paper clips, and envelopes with yellowed flaps. Business cards of people who could have been dead by now. Broken umbrellas, tattered slippers she missed when she first moved in. She wanted to leave the apartment with less junk than it had at the beginning of the summer.

Her phone rang as she opened a second plastic garbage bag. It was her husband's ring. The Perry Mason theme song. He never called her at this time. It must be really late at night the day before.

She ran into the living room and picked up the phone from the coffee table.

"Hi," she said, a little out of breath.

"You know how Piaf gets when you're away?" her husband asked.

"Neurotic?"

"Sick."

"What do you mean, sick?" She felt her heart beating in her throat. "Tell me she's okay."

"Piaf's fine. She just spent a couple of days at the vet."

"What happened?"

"Hot peppers in something she ate."

"You fed her hot peppers?

"Not on purpose. It was take-out chicken. She couldn't resist it, and I thought I'd gotten rid of all the peppers."

"That's terrifying."

"Yes, she misses you. She's very happy now. I think she really wanted to die."

"You know you don't have to give me the details. You really didn't have to tell me that."

"Your eldest kid would have. You know how Ted loves to pull your chain."

"Is this to make me feel guilty?"

"Why should you feel guilty? You haven't fallen in love with some guy there have you?"

"Don't make me laugh," she said and blushed. "I'm ancient."

"Not to me."

"I'm glad she's feeling okay."

"Piaf's all better. That's why I told you."

"I still think it's to make me feel guilty."

"See you soon, honey," he said.

"Yes, very soon."

SEVENTY-FOUR

The train to Sendai was so fast she could only see electric lines as they flashed by the landscape. Suddenly she felt like lightning might strike again and she didn't know what she'd do if it happened and she was so far away from home. The heat gave her headaches and did weird things to her eyes. She drank lots of water and tried to not get too tired, but often she was afraid that in a split second everything could change.

She closed her eyes and fell asleep. She felt safe with Richard sitting next to her. He was reading. When she opened her eyes, they were almost at Sendai.

"Feeling better?" he asked.

"Much better," she said. "I haven't been sleeping very much. The trucks wake me up."

They drove down the coast past the towns wedged below the mountains on the edge of the Pacific Ocean. How strange, she thought, she could see northern California if the air was clear enough. Impossible, Richard said, there's the curvature of the Earth and that would erase whatever bump you get from the clarity of the air.

From the road above the towns, they could see uneven roofs, metal sheds, or fancier houses with several tiled gables. Sometimes the roads dropped down near the ocean and there were beaches of gray sand. Fishing boats in clusters in the harbor, or one or two farther out to sea. Squid fishermen, Richard said.

There were fields full of flowers planted in rows. Sunflowers and red Gerbera daisies. Gardens of ripening cabbages and eggplants. Rice fields shimmering green. Egrets fished in shallow water.

Was it selfish to be elated – a word that came easily suddenly – that she was sitting in a tiny red car driving toward a place demolished by wind and water and fire not that long ago? She'd read that for years scientists had tried to tame lightning to understand matter. Lightning had more voltage than any other natural thing. She was born again by the lightning in her brain, she thought.

She wasn't one of those people who stopped their cars to see an accident on the highway, was she? Maybe it was just the sense that she'd escaped something and gotten away almost scot-free, though she hadn't felt that carefree when she was home. She was distracted by Richard's arm on the steering wheel. She wanted to run her finger on his skin. She couldn't remember the last time she noticed her husband's hands or his mouth or his arms. He was so much a part of her.

They pulled up to a gas station with a large sign suspended on white pillars. The sign was bright red and stood out against the cloudless sky.

"This sign is famous," Richard said. "It says that the water was as high as the sign, 15.1 meters after 3/11. The gas station vanished but the sign was still here. They rebuilt it a year after the quake."

"Why did they keep the sign?"

"To remember the horror, the owner said. There was nothing here. For months, thousands of people were missing."

"Oh," she said. And felt guilty for being happy when she was in the place now where almost everything had disappeared.

"Do you think Motoko is right?"

"Yes and no. It's important to see what happened. How the villages and cities have survived. To continue to bear witness to the loss."

"Why?"

"We can never really understand, I suppose, but I'm so oblivious, I think, most of the time in Tokyo. It seems like a joke, wild boar taking over, but it's something very different. Unpredictable."

The word unpredictable repeated like a gong in her head. Life is unpredictable. Kids are unpredictable.

"Yes," she said, "like being a parent. My sons are always surprising me. Do you worry about your kids?" Gigi asked.

Richard didn't answer her at first. Finally, he said, "Not so much anymore. How about you?"

"Constantly," she said and shrugged.

They stopped to buy food in a village that was still miles away from the town where Richard's friend used to live. Would the wild boar come running out of the houses? She wondered if it would be like feeding the deer in the holy city.

Richard filled a basket with food, as if they were on a longer trip than she imagined.

"First, a reconnaissance," he said. "I'll do a little bit of exploring with the Geiger counter while you sit in the car, so we can figure out how safe it is."

Was all that food for her? She wondered. Was it like a stakeout or something, waiting for the radioactive boar to appear?

"*Sayonara*," the woman at the checkout counter said. She'd emptied Gigi's change purse into the machine that counted out coins and then clucked at her.

Gigi had said, "*Konnichiwa*," and that's when the woman said, "*Sayonara*," as if that word was a better word for the situation. It was something Gigi needed at that minute. To be encouraged to find the right word, even though the months she struggled to find any words at all were still quite raw. Their kitchen had been covered with post-it notes. Knife, spoon, milk, drawer. Like learning a new language.

Gigi walked along the grass bordering the road and saw a woman with a tiny dog on a leash walking toward her. A small brown dog with curly fur. A toy poodle. She squatted down to pet the poodle's head and the dog licked her hand and put her tiny feet on Gigi's knee. She was so trusting.

"Where are you from?" the woman asked. She told her the truth, though she wanted to say planet nowhere. And she wanted to add, "I'm traveling with a man I hardly know thousands of miles away from my family who I love into the place with the radioactive boar."

There were no wild boar when they drove into the empty town. It was noon. They'd wound around the headland and onto the road following the shore. She'd imagined something else. A wilderness. Mangy dogs were lying in the sun. Monkeys disappeared into thickets along the side of the road as they drove by. Magpies flicked their long gray and white tails on fence posts. Along the edges of the road, someone had planted sunflowers.

"It's weird," she said. "Really weird to see how empty it all is." Pompoms of twisted branches surrounded the old wooden houses.

Richard said, "For years I didn't think about the nuclear attacks. How silent those cities must have been. I've been looking at maps of the bomb blast. The Hiroshima Peace Museum had an exhibit of photographs not long ago. The photographer died, but an RAF pilot, who was there six months later, bought the camera. His son found the pictures after all these years. Most everything is demolished. Only a Torii gate left standing."

"I suppose no one wants to think about what we did," Gigi said.

"No. There's one pretty devastating picture of a mother feeding her child. Her face is streaked with blood."

"So heartbreaking."

"In another photo, a mother and her child are standing holding pieces of bread just hours after the blast. The mother's face is wrapped in bandages."

They opened the car windows, though she wasn't so sure that was a good idea in case the radiation was still high enough to hurt them. The surf pounded the beach. It was hot. The air conditioning had stopped feeling like cool air, and the breeze from the ocean was a relief.

"We'll stop soon," Richard said, "and I'll walk around a bit and test the readings. The radiation is probably at different levels in the soil depending on where we are"

"What about me?" Gigi asked.

"It's probably safer for you to stay in the car."

It seemed like an illogical thing for a physicist to say. After all, they'd been riding with the windows open. Molecules bouncing off the ground would have mixed with the air in the car, she thought.

SEVENTY-FIVE

She watched Richard snap the switch on the hand-held Geiger counter and press it into the ground near where he had parked the car. The device beeped incessantly.

She was thinking about a woman she'd seen the day before as she walked home from the university. She was dressed in a black kimono. Her obi was flowered, blue and white, and she carried her bamboo basket on her left arm. There was an off-white cloth covering the top of the basket. She was walking slowly. Gigi watched her totter on her geta in the heat. She swayed back and forth. She could see the nape of her neck, a gold clasp in her hair twisted on her head. She held a pale green umbrella with her right hand. She was close behind her and she smelled the clean smell of her hair. Like lavender. She knew she'd have to pass her. She was too close. Too curious about her life.

She promised herself that she'd look back and see her face once she

220   SHARON WHITE

got to the steps of her building, but when she turned, the woman had vanished. She was gone in two minutes, disappeared. Evaporated. Gigi thought for a minute she might have imagined her.

Her phone dinged and she pulled her bag onto her lap and fished it out. Mom, the text read, I'm okay but call me. Got to tell you something. It was her younger son. The son she loved above all else she thought. Though she loved her older son and her husband too. This son needed more love sometimes. She listened to the silence as the different satellites, or whatever they were, lined up so she could talk to her son in the early morning the day before. It was like time travel.

"I fell off my loft," he said.

"Oh no," she said.

"But I'm fine. Just not so beautiful."

"This isn't funny," she said.

"I know, Mom, but I spent most of the day yesterday in the emergency room and I'm fine. The eye surgeon said the scar won't even show, she was careful to hide it in the fold. The nurse thought it was a knife fight."

"How did it happen? You weren't drinking, were you?"

"No Mom. I rolled over and must've fallen out onto the ladder. I woke up and there was blood everywhere."

"I told your father that metal ladder was dangerous," she said.

"For once, your paranoid fears were right."

She could see Richard coming back toward the car. He was looking cheerful. Why did he always look either cheerful or zoned out?

"Are you sure you're okay?"

"Yes," he said, "but Mom..."

"Yes?"

"I miss you."

She smiled, but he couldn't see it.

"Let's talk tomorrow. Are you sure they checked your head?"

"No concussion," he said.

She didn't say it, but what about that famous actress everyone thought was okay after a skiing accident and then she died the next day? She fell on such an easy slope, one that even a toddler could ski.

Richard said, "The radiation levels seem safe but I'm not sure what they'll be like closer to Fukushima," he said and put the Geiger counter on the back seat.

They saw a truck pull out of a side road as they headed south. The driver was gesturing to the man beside him. They seemed to be having an argument.

The truck was a livestock van, slats on the sides for air. Maybe she was right after all that someone was importing radioactive boar from this part of the prefecture.

SEVENTY-SIX

When they drove into the driveway of the house where Richard's friend grew up, the sun was beating down on the car.

Even north of Tokyo the heat followed them. The house was perched high above the water. His friend's family must have been able to see the tsunami crashing into the town below, splintering the pines with their bristly tips and the clipped bushes around the harbor and the cars lined up in the parking spaces.

They were not far from a school, still empty, Richard told her.

"The government's insisting it's safe to return. I know I wouldn't rush to come back. I guess there's no way to predict how many of the people who once lived here will move back. They must have new lives now."

The door was unlocked and Richard turned the handle carefully.

"My friend hasn't come back to check things out. He said he didn't want to see what a mess it was."

There was a wooden bowl on the counter, a bowl that once probably had fruit in it. The counter was dusty and papers were scattered on the floor. Everything was so neat, really, not at all like the pictures she'd seen of cities torn apart by the tsunami, evacuated after the reactor flooded. There was no sign of animals yet.

"The high-water mark was just below here," Richard said. "We can walk up later to the shrine at the top of the hill."

At the edge of the terraced field below them they could see a white truck. The driver had pulled the truck into the flat area near a shed. Something that was once a garden. He got out of the cab and another man hopped out. Punk yakuza types, Richard said. The men wore black t-shirts and jeans, aggressive tattoos snaking around their arms. They stood talking.

It was a small livestock truck with a drawing of a cow and a pig high-fiving on the side. "What's written on the truck?" Gigi asked.

"Fine Meat," Richard said. "Pretty ironic, isn't it? That's a Tokyo phone number under

the drawing. Maybe you're right. They are selling wild boar to restaurants in the city. Radioactive boar."

The men were arguing as they walked away from the truck toward the village.

"They won't find anything to eat, if that's what they want."

"Just the vending machine," Gigi smiled.

"Once they lifted the ban on the city, the company must have started restocking the machines."

Richard put his hand on Gigi's arm. "You're clammy."

"Is that supposed to be a compliment?"

"Not quite. You need more water. I think hiking up to the shrine's probably not such a good idea."

She nodded.

"Let's go check out that truck."

"But aren't they yakuza?"

"Maybe," he said, "though they like you to call them ninkyo dan-tai."

"Why?"

"It hurts their feelings if you think they're gangsters. They see themselves as knights."

"I don't think so," she said. "Do you?"

Richard laughed. "What do you think?"

They walked quickly down the gravel road to where the truck was parked. They'd changed into their other shoes in case the soil was contaminated enough to be a problem. The levels were the same as they'd been at the convenience store. When they got close enough, they could see the snouts of wild boar poking against the mesh on the sides of the truck. They were fierce looking and smelled rank.

"But they'll all be slaughtered, won't they?"

"Yes," he said. "But the government's been killing them all over the prefecture. I suppose this is almost the same fate, except for the long ride in the steaming truck."

"What would happen if we let them out?" she said.

"You'll be close enough to touch them, if they don't run you down first or bite your fingers off."

Gigi walked to the back of the truck and fiddled with the latches on the ramp.

"You don't think we're really going to do this?"

"Why not," she said.

"Because it's dangerous."

"Haven't you wanted to do something like this?"

"Not now," he said. "Maybe when I was younger. It's irresponsible."

"You feel responsible?"

"Yes. I don't want anyone to get hurt. Step away from the truck and we'll go get some water and think about climbing up to the shrine. We may be able to see some boar in the forest. It's full of boar."

"You don't like feeling out of control?

"No. I don't want you to get hurt."

They could hear the boar grunting and snuffling. "No," she said. "It's tragic they're caught in the truck."

It was as if all those years of rehab and anguish had caught up to her standing in the hot sun. She could imagine how the boar felt, trapped in the stifling truck.

Richard moved closer to her and said, "No? We don't know how many there are or how riled. Or what they'll do. They're wild and angry. Fierce."

She didn't know why she was being so obstinate, a word she'd never have been able to call up a few years ago. It was a triumph to say it with conviction even to herself. She didn't like Richard feeling responsible for her. She was tired of everyone holding their arms out to protect her. She was hardly ever afraid of anything before her stroke. Now she was determined to do something to help the boar. They were huffing at the mesh on the side of the truck. She liked their gamey smell. She felt sorry for them.

It was easy to spring the latches on the ramp. It clattered to the ground. She climbed up and released the lock on the roll-up door. One boar pressed against the mesh webbing gate. He was big. Two hundred pounds, she guessed, and his snout was curved up like the tiny netsuke in the museum. The others were blinking in the dim trailer. There were several large boar. She was surprised to see there were piglets, too. They were squealing. Their backs were spotted like fawns. There was a nest of hay in the back of the trailer. They must have been terrified when the two men rounded them up and herded them into the truck.

"You see they've captured a whole family," she said. "If I had a bucket of food I could coax them out."

"Ah," he said. "Once we open this gate, they'll follow the leader out."

She was surprised when he helped her release the mesh barrier. "Don't get near them."

But she'd already moved out of the way.

Three of the boar trotted down the metal incline and when they got to the bottom they turned and ran up to the field.

They looked harmless, though she knew they'd been scavenging in empty towns and in newly planted fields. She could see there were two more adults and four piglets with tan colored skin in the truck. Their white stripes glowed in the bright light. Soon they were clattering down the ramp.

One of the piglets sniffed her legs and snorted. Gigi laughed. Then it ran after the other piglets who were galloping toward their mother.

They had bristly hides and glinting eyes, but there weren't twenty, as they had guessed from the size of the truck. The animals had wanted to get away from them as fast as they could, once they stood blinking for a few seconds in the darkness of the trailer.

No one was growing crops in the fields now, but zucchini had self-seeded. The adults were headed towards the swollen zucchini. The boar were huge, as big as ottomans. Their ears were small and furry.

Gigi sat down in the long grass and crossed her legs. Bees dipped past her face buzzing the wildflowers. Daisies and small orange lilies. Such ordinary flowers. The bees' legs were thick with pollen. There were blue butterflies in the grass.

The boar had stopped to eat the long weeds. Two were devouring the zucchini. The piglets scampered in the matted field like puppies. The air was sweet and a small breeze had come up. Seagulls swooped above the field.

She felt a great sense of relief. She'd opened the metal door for them. She was sitting in a field as far away as she'd ever been from her family. She was alive and the boar were snuffling and whistling in the abandoned field. All around her, years of cultivation had disappeared. They were all doing the best they could. She was doing the best she could.

And then she started to cry. She hated crying. She couldn't catch her breath and she was mortified that Richard would see her crying. She hadn't saved the boar. She'd only postponed their death. She wiped her eyes and nose with her sleeve. But at least she'd done something.

Richard squatted beside her. His face was damp. He ran his hand over his forehead.

"They look happy," he said. "But you don't." He touched her shoulder.

"Will the men know we're the ones who let the boar go?"

"Only if they see us," he said. "If we move quickly, we can get into the house before they get back to the truck."

"Are they dangerous?"

"They could be. I shouldn't have suggested we check this out. I didn't know we'd end up doing something like this."

He helped her up and they ran up the hill to his friend's house and pushed the door open. She stepped over tattered shoji and rumpled clothes. Sadness had scattered the remnants of this family.

Gigi felt a hand on her neck. Where was Richard? He'd gone into the kitchen to make tea, even though it was very hot and she felt as if she couldn't breathe. The boar were still in the field eating the zucchini. They looked happy, their snouts pushed into the ripe flesh. She thought the yakuza were safely eating lunch. Richard would never put his hands on her neck.

"Don't move," the man said. Why was he speaking English? His hand was covered with the tattoos she'd seen from quite far away on his arms. Bright blue and red dragon scales. He'd wound his gray hair into a man bun. He pushed her into the kitchen and Richard turned around slowly. She had no idea if he'd do anything to save her if it came to that.

It was like a movie. She was a step away from herself. Watchful. Not quite in charge. A kind of out of body experience.

"Sit down on the floor," he said, motioning to Richard and then he pushed her down next to him. Their backs were against the cabinets. It was amazing to her that the house had survived the tsunami. Everything was pretty much intact.

A cup on the counter, packages of noodles on the shelves. A can in the open refrigerator, full of mold.

Chopsticks in the open drawers.

The yakuza had a sushi knife in his belt and she was hoping Richard would not try anything heroic. The man pulled his arm back like he was throwing a ball and then slapped Richard across the face. She felt the slap in her throat—a kind of reverberation. She was afraid for a minute that she was next.

The man took some zip ties from his pocket and wrapped their wrists behind them and then tied their ankles.

He said something in Japanese to Richard and then turned and walked out of the house.

They could hear him talking to the other yakuza and then the truck started and pulled away.

"What did he say to you?" she asked.

"That was a stupid thing we did, but not enough to die for. He had to tie us up so he wouldn't lose face with his friend. Are you okay?"

"Yes," she said. "Your face is starting to bruise."

"I've had lots worse."

She wanted to feel something more than just relief that she was alive. That she could talk and walk and do all those things she took for granted before her stroke. Now she was in a place where a kind of resurrection had followed destruction. She was fiddling with the zip ties behind her back. They were the kind her husband used to organize his computer cords.

"We may be able to just slip them off," she said.

"There's a knife here somewhere." Richard shifted his legs on the floor. He hitched himself up and hopped along the counter until he found a drawer with knives.

By that time, she'd wiggled free. She stood up and said, "Here, I'll get yours." She chose a small knife and cut the ties off his wrists.

"I was afraid he was going to really beat you up."

"He just needed to let me know he was the boss. He was angry because they'd hired someone to capture the boar and now that money is lost. The boar are not easy to catch. They're very fast if they want to get away. There are hundreds in the mountains but they're almost impossible to find there."

SEVENTY-SEVEN

They stumbled out into the bright light and looked down at the empty town.

Everything was still. It was a beautiful day. She knew Richard wasn't happy she'd put them in danger, but he seemed strangely exhilarated after their brush with the ninkyo dantai.

"They're probably retired and must be desperate for cash if they're transporting so few boar into the city. Or else someone's paying more than they should for wild meat. Let's walk down to that vending machine and get something cold to drink," he said.

"Sure," Gigi said.

"I think I've been irresponsible in encouraging you to come with me."

"I'm an adult," she said.

"You're pretty calm."

"Not so calm. Just thinking. I won't have another stroke if that's what you're wondering. Everything's just caught up to me."

He'd probably seen her crying in the field. How could he know how stable she was? Maybe he thought she was having a breakdown.

"It's so sad," she said. "No one living in these houses. No one cultivating rice or gathering ripe plums."

Gigi turned and started walking down the steep hill. "Something cold's a great idea. I'm really hot."

When they got near enough to the vending machine, they could see a middle-aged man stocking the slots. He wore a green cap and wiped the sweat from his face.

"I'll be finished soon, *gaijin*," he said, and then laughed. "You from Tokyo? Some of those tourists?"

"No," Richard said, "what tourists?"

"Some new thing," he said and closed the door. "I think there's only been five or so of them in little vans. I used to live in a beautiful house on the hill. I was a rich guy once. But I lost everything in the tsunami."

"I'm sorry," Gigi said.

"You sorry? I'm really sorry, too. But I saved my granddaughter. She was only two. Here," he said and handed them two cold orange drinks from his truck.

"*Arigato*," Richard said.

A woman was coming toward the man as he opened the cab of his truck. She was walking with a cane. Her gray hair was pulled up in a twist on her head. She smiled at the workman. He turned and waved at her and then he stepped up into the cab. Soon he was gone and she came closer and closer to where they were standing.

"I have some tea for you," she said to Richard, "and some sweet buns." She bowed and said, "Himari."

Richard bowed and said, "That's very kind." He turned to Gigi. "This is Gigi and I'm Richard."

They followed her slowly down the paved road, the electrical wires swinging above their heads, past rice fields overgrown with tangled weeds. They passed a car covered with vines. She motioned to an open doorway and they took their shoes off and put on the soft slippers lined up near the step. There was a television on in the first room and a very old man sat in a chair watching a baseball game. On a low table in the corner of the next room she'd set out a pot of tea and a plate of shiny buns.

"It was my *ryokan*," she said.

"You must have been very busy before the disaster," Richard said.

"Yes, but now no one comes except Toshio who stocks the machine. I was one of the few in town who lived. And my father and I are the only ones here. I didn't want to live in those rows of tiny sheds they put all my neighbors into. My father was visiting a friend in Tokyo and when he heard I was alive he wanted to come back here. You know it started to snow, after everything that happened that day there was snow on my eyelashes. I'd waded through waist deep black water and saw my daughter pulled out to sea and saw my husband float away with the top of the house, but I held tightly to a staircase I found still standing. I sank again and again in the muddy current until I pulled myself out. And the next morning I was able to walk the mountain path to the next village where people were gathered in the temple. I didn't want to live at that point and the snow was on my tongue and in my eyes and covering my hands. I couldn't stop shivering and no one knew who I was. Everyone I knew had died."

"I'm so sorry," Gigi said. "Does someone check on you and your father here?"

"Oh yes. It turns out my niece was okay. She lived in a village not far from here and tried to get me to move with her to Tokyo, but I couldn't see myself away from this place. My great grandfather was the one who built the house and it seemed like a sign that I should stay, since a good part of it remained. Chiyo makes sure I have food and that I'm still well. And I have this," she said and smiled as she took a cell phone out of her large pocket.

"Why not stay here?" Himari-san said. She smiled at Gigi. "It is too late for you to drive to Sendai and get the train. I have a nice room in good shape in case someone like you shows up."

Gigi excused herself and went out of the room where Richard and Himari-san were still talking and drinking more tea. She'd started to shake. Her legs bounced together, and she had a hard time keeping her teeth from chattering.

She walked into the room near the door and sat down on a stool next to the old man watching television. She held her legs to steady them.

He pointed to the screen and said, "baseballru."

It was the Giants playing the Toyo Carp.

"Good game?" She gave him a thumbs up.

The old man shook his head and pointed at the score line on the screen. The Giants were losing.

"I saw Ichiro play for the Yankees."

Himari-san's father laughed and nodded his head. "Very great hitter," he said and held his hands out clasped around an invisible bat.

Can you get two rooms?" she asked Richard when he stuck his head around the doorway.

"We'll see," he said.

But after a few minutes, Himari-san led them through the *ryokan* down a long hall where there were flowers arranged in a basket on the wall. Ikebana. She studied the form of the flowers for a minute. White branches for the main line, a pink tropical flower at the base, and a spray of deep green leaves against the wall.

They had a beautiful room, she had to admit. But the immaculate

SHARON WHITE

futons were set out quite close to each other and there was a white dragon at their heads in an alcove with a print of misty green mountains. A low table was positioned in front of the shoji. There were two low seats with embroidered pillows.

"You're cold," Himari-san said and opened a large cupboard where there was a white sweater hanging. "Put it on."

She held the sweater as Gigi put her arms through the sleeves.

"*Arigato*," Gigi said and smiled.

"You were too wild. But it is because you are kind." She turned and walked down the hall.

The room had paper walls. Gigi felt like she was entombed in an ivory box until she pulled the shoji aside and there was a window.

When Richard had gone to the toilet, she pulled one of the futons closer to the wall.

Before their encounter with the wild boar and the yakuza she'd been imagining they'd book one room in whatever hotel they found, and he would bend and flick the feathery duvet away and bend again to touch her face with his lips and then slip her top off and then kiss her breasts and then her stomach and then — And she wouldn't have to think about anything for several moments, not anything at all. She could taste his lips against hers. The pressure of his body. No loss, no misplaced words.

But instead, she just wanted to stop shaking.

When Richard came back into the room he pushed his hair back from his forehead and said, "Sorry about this. It's the only room that was clean."

"It's okay. I wanted to stay in a ryokan."

"You're still shaking," he said. "Himari-san is worried about you. Her father told her you must have had a bad fright."

"I'm fine. I'll take a hot shower. It's the whole day. It's caught up to me. I'll be fine."

The shower was in a narrow room next to the bath one step down from their room. She pulled her clothes off and stood under the water for a long time.

She changed into pajamas in the tiny room with the toilet. By the time she was finished, he was on his futon with his chin propped up on his hand and the duvet pulled up.

"Feel better now?"

She nodded.

"I'm sorry it's been such a difficult day."

"It felt like one of those caper movies," she said as she got into her futon and pulled up the flowered quilt. "The whole day's been surreal. So much tragedy but in a ghost town. But this is something different."

She gestured to the dragon and the painting. "She's very generous."

Richard smiled but he looked incredibly sad. He shifted a bit in his bed and said, "I always wanted to go off to the wilderness. In high school it was the West. I talked my cousin Harry into driving to Oregon, three days driving nonstop. It was so wild out there. Madrona blocking the way to the beach. Camping near the water even though it was illegal. It was so different from where we were from, growing up in a town not far away from a place with perpetual underground fires. The catacombs of coal mining. I used to feel hemmed in even growing up. That's probably why I ended up moving away. If I'd stayed, I would've ended up in jail, since that's where most of my relatives worked."

"And then you studied physics," Gigi said.

"It was a language I could understand. It translated wilderness into numbers. There was something comforting in that. There was still mystery in the world. You approached any problem by reducing it to the simplest case imaginable. You could miss some details and, later, calculate refinements to capture the essence of the real world."

She propped her head up with her pillow. She was warm now. He was telling her a bedtime story. She closed her eyes.

"When I was a kid I'd spend weekends with my grandparents, in the hills near the burning town. They were such simple people. My grandfather had horses and a few cows, and my grandmother raised chickens. It was pretty idyllic, though they were really dirt poor and knew it. My parents weren't in much better shape. My father was a car salesman and my mother taught kindergarten. I loved the horses. I was pretty good at riding one small white horse around the little corral my grandfather made. I pretended I was a cowboy."

"Hmmm," she said.

"Sleep well," he said and turned away from her.

But he talked in his sleep and she tossed and turned. She was worried about her son. Even when Richard was mumbling he disappeared. He seemed insubstantial, and when she dreamed the dragon had clamped down on her head, there was no one to help her escape. She'd hardly slept at all.

They were so close to the coast and the light was blazing. A soft insistence not like anything she'd seen before.

He woke up as Gigi was texting her son.

Still okay? she typed.

Great mom. Don't worry. I'm fine.

Love you.

Love you too.

R ichard pulled the duvet off. He was wearing shorts and a t-shirt. He washed his face at the sink in the hall near the room. His white hair slicked back.

"Trouble?"

"My younger son fell off the loft in his apartment and sliced his eyelid open."

"Wow. He's okay?"

"He says he is, but I never know with him."

"We should go down to breakfast. Himari-san told me her niece brought food not long ago."

"But should we eat her food?"

"We'll have to," he said. "It will hurt her feelings if we don't. We can give her some of the food we bought for the trip before we leave. She told me when she was in the evacuation center they had two slices of apple, one rice ball, and a bottle of juice at night. But people were happy to have anything to eat. Many had survived for days without food."

The low table was set with small dishes of little pickles, salmon slices, rice strewn with seaweed, tiny fish in a cup, squares of cooked egg, peppers sliced thin. The tea steamed on a red lacquer tray near black bowls and chopsticks. Where had she found the flowers in the alcove? An arrangement of pink lilies and ferns.

They were perfectly quiet and they stayed that way until Himari-san came back and asked Richard something in Japanese.

"She wants to know if we'd like more tea."

When Gigi was in the ancient country so many years ago she knew some Japanese. And she could almost speak to the man she thought she loved in his language. But all those words had vanished over the years.

"We have to get going," Gigi said. "We've got the drive and getting the car back." She was almost embarrassed to have spent such an intimate night with him that wasn't intimate at all. Or was it? And she thought about him as a little boy riding a white horse in his grandfather's dusty corral.

He nodded and said something to their host. Himari-san bowed and turned away.

SEVENTY-EIGHT

They drove back to Sendai past the towns devastated by the disasters of 3/11. Battered by earthquake and wave and radiation. Himari-san told them the people in the village had waited years to rebuild and by the time they got permission, they'd moved to Tokyo or to the houses of their children.

"We're too polite," she said, "we need to be louder so the government hears us."

Farmers were bent over rice growing in terraces along the mountains. Tending to their fields. Lilies were about to bloom in their neat rows in some of the fields.

"You know we live with sorrow, but happiness can still be real," Himari-san said, patting Richard's shoulder when they left.

When they got back to the city after their trip, they were exhausted. They expected a wilderness teeming with life, but instead the devastation was all around them.

They both felt a little foolish; they weren't even worth killing to the ninkyo dantai. Not a threat at all. Maybe, Richard said, their business with the boar was not really something the yakuza cared about. A sideline. Something to laugh about. The yakuza probably figured they wouldn't report the incident and what would the police do? Everyone was paid off to do nothing. These groups were really powerful.

Maybe the men they encountered weren't even active, but in some other profession. The government had cracked down on businesses working with gang members a few years before. He told Gigi he'd read some ex-yakuza had even taken up acting. They thought their families would accept them as hardworking if they knew they were in showbiz, one man said.

SEVENTY-NINE

It felt like she'd just dropped off to sleep when she heard a rap on the door and then another. The bedroom was lit with the lights from the buildings across the canal. She walked down the narrow hallway and stood at the door waiting. Maybe it was a dream. Who's there, she said. It's me, Richard said.

She unlocked the door, the bolts snapping as she opened it. He was standing just steps away. His face was creased with sleep.

"I had a bad dream."

"Are you sleepwalking?"

"I don't think so."

"Do you want to come in?"

"No, I don't think so."

Her feet were cold, she was starting to feel as if she were dreaming.

He sat down on the linoleum floor in the corridor and folded his legs under him.

She said, "Are you sure you don't want to come in? I can make some tea. What was the dream about?"

"I pulled the weeds away from the green phone booth outside the building and opened the door," he said.

"Inside the box it was dark. I picked up the phone and dialed a number I seemed to know by heart. Directions to a village high in the mountains. Sacred. It was very cold there and once I was on the trail I realized I should've brought my heavier coat, the one with the hood. The houses were wooden with peaked roofs. The wind was blowing and I opened the door to the largest house I could find. I knew they grew tobacco here in the high valley and dried the leaves in the rafters of the houses. The floor was covered with the pulverized dust of the leaves. They'd find my footprints in the morning in the valuable tobacco. Someone was ringing a hollow bell in the village. I was supposed to find someone I loved in a temple the next valley over, but I knew it would take hours to get there in the wind. I couldn't figure out why I couldn't move my feet. Why my heart was beating at all if I was in a place where I could find this person who had died years ago. I trudged across the narrow spine of the mountain, snow blasting my face. My fingers were frozen and ice coated my eyelashes. How would he know who I was in the dark and wind?"

She touched his arm. "Was it someone you loved very much?"

"Yes."

"Want to talk about it?"

"No, I don't think so. Some time," he said. "I feel pretty stupid right now."

She laughed. "I think we look cute leaning against the wall here, whispering. Come in for some tea now?"

"No," he said and stood. "It's just something that happens now and then, these dreams."

EIGHTY

Richard was telling her about nirvana as she speared a radish cut into the shape of a flower and dipped it in the bubbling pot of fish goo. They'd done something different and met in the lobby of their building.

He was wearing a black shirt. A little strange for him and she'd spent ten minutes trying to decide what to wear. It felt like a date and she was nervous about that. But really, they were just going to the restaurant on the patio across from their apartments. The restaurant served pizza and a strange mix of Japanese and Italian food like a few other restaurants in their neighborhood. The owner, a tall woman with heavy eyeliner at the edges of her eyes, was not happy to see them, not happy at all. At first she said they had no tables and then Richard said something to her in Japanese and she backed up a step and pointed to a table by a window set for two. It was reserved, he told

Gigi, and now it's not.

"Once we have our eyes, ears, tongue we make contact with the sensory world," Richard said, "and then feelings arise. And once we have feelings, tanha bubbles up. We crave pleasant feelings and we crave to escape unpleasant feelings. There's a battle between feeling and craving. We decide whether bondage will continue forever or if it will be replaced by enlightenment. You give up the driving thirst for pleasure. You're free, then, from perpetual rebirth."

He picked up a slice of zucchini with his fingers and moved it around in the bubbling liquid. It was like a lava lamp, the oil popping up with a snap.

"There are two kinds of nirvana, the first we experience here and then the second after our final death."

"So how do we reach nirvana?" she asked.

"Mindfulness," he said, smiling. And then he took a bite of the zucchini slice. "Meditation. We cultivate an awareness of our feelings. Everything around us makes us feel something."

"We don't want to feel, then," she said and pulled her skirt down across her knees.

"You don't want to be caught in your reactions to the world. If you pay attention you can escape the craving."

"And have you reached nirvana?" she asked as the owner took away the bubbling pot and replaced it a few seconds later with plates of spaghetti laced with basil and tiny tomatoes.

"No," he said, "but that's not really the point for me."

The other tables were full of salarymen stopping to eat after work. They were loud, laughing and sharing big plates of food. She watched as they carefully poured each other glasses of beer. To be polite, Motoko had told her. Every now and then the men would glance over at their table.

EIGHTY-ONE

The afternoon light flooded into Richard's apartment. She'd met his daughter Amanda in the lobby and she had invited Gigi to tea. She'd gone out to dinner with Richard and his daughter the night before. They'd walked down the path along the lit canal to the Greek restaurant perched on the edge of the water and eaten fish and chips together.

His daughter told Gigi that her father was a huge disappointment. Richard worked long hours when his kids needed him, what with the short attention span of their mother and the mess in the house. Well, not really a *mess*, but no one in her family really took care of anyone else.

"That's why Dad went all Zen on us," she said, and offered Gigi another cookie. Gigi put her hand into the bag and pulled out a cookie she'd eaten since she was a teenager. Chessmen. How strange that you could buy those cookies here.

"It's because of all the expats in this neighborhood," Amanda said. "Haven't you seen them?"

Gigi shook her head.

Sometimes she felt like she didn't see, really see, most of what was around her. She needed to be woken and woken again. Like those days she spent in Tokyo years before with the poet, his long hair tied in a cord at his neck. The fragrant trumpets of datura opening below the window on the canal.

Amanda looked out at the water. She was tall, like Richard, and slim. Gigi never understood it when people told her that her sons looked just like her husband, even though they had her eyes. She couldn't see the resemblance.

Gigi said, "Tell me about your brother."

"Dad didn't tell you anything about him?"

Amanda pointed at the photograph on the little shrine on a shelf above the desk.

"Not really," Gigi said. "He talks more about you. He told me his son loved reading and camping when he was young, but he didn't go into a lot of details."

"Curt. His name is Curt. And he's been dead for over ten years."

Gigi got up from the sofa and walked over to the desk. She leaned closer to look at the photo and then picked it up. She ran her finger over the glass and then put it back on the shelf.

She felt cold all over and then a rush of sadness moved through her. She closed her eyes for a minute, and then she turned around and looked at Richard's daughter. "I don't know what to say. It must have been so awful for you."

Amanda said, "Yes. It was. Maybe Dad didn't want to make you unhappy. But that's my father. Not exactly an open book."

Gigi was surprised his daughter could see how she felt. Diminished, left out.

"I know he cares about you," she said.

Richard had kept so much of his life from her. She'd been proud of herself that she could open up with someone she didn't really know when she'd been so protected by her family. But it turned out most people really didn't want to hear about her stroke. They had their own problems. But Richard had seemed different.

In the photo, his son was on top of Fuji gazing off into the sky, away from the photographer. You could see the curved roof of a shrine in the corner of the photo. His profile looked a bit like Richard's. Thoughtful, kind. But what could you tell from a photograph?

Amanda pulled the sliding glass door closed and turned on the air conditioning.

"Curt came to Japan to see Dad and to squeeze in some skiing. He'd been in a horrific car crash a few years before and then recovered after months in the hospital. I think he wanted to reconnect with my father. And he loved skiing. He was out of bounds at Hakuba, this ski area about three hours away by train. There'd been a big snow dump, so he took an overnight bus and planned on skiing for a day and then taking the train back. He thought it was so great you could get where you wanted to go in a flash.

"He knew all about avalanche protocols and had all the gear. An avalanche beacon, a shovel and a probe. He'd told Dad where he'd be skiing and Dad had no qualms about it even though it was very wild there. Curt sent me an email with incredible shots of the mountains. He was a professional photographer. I miss him a lot. We were pretty close since our parents were kind of consumed by their own stuff."

Gigi walked over to the sliding glass door and looked down at the canal. She could almost see the bay from his balcony. She was hurt that he'd kept this shattering loss from her. She'd confessed so much to him.

"It was a freak avalanche. The conditions should have been safe, but the whole bowl slid. And the strange thing was, it happened on the same day as the earthquake and tsunami on the coast. The ski patrol searched for him, but never found his body. They thought it could have been tremors from the earthquake that set it off. And there was so much going on that day, who knows."

Amanda shrugged and poured more tea into their cups.

"After the avalanche, a young priest from the Zen temple on the mountain told Dad not to worry, he'd perform a funeral service for Curt, even though they'd never found his body. The priest gave Dad a memorial tablet. An ihai. He said Curt was renamed so he could be reborn. He didn't want Dad to grieve forever that his soul was lost. Mom still hasn't forgiven Dad for letting Curt go off on his own to ski. She hired a rescue team to search for his body in the summer. She was fucking nuts about the whole thing. She wouldn't stop until they'd searched under every rock in the area. But it was useless. The whole side of the mountain had slid."

"How terrible for your family," Gigi said and sat back down on the couch. Her hands were shaking. She put one over the other in her lap.

"You don't get over something like that, do you? Dad thought, if only Curt hadn't been an adrenaline junky, he might have lived to be old, very old. People in our family often live past ninety. I think he feels guilty. Curt was always pushing himself. He wanted Dad to think he was a big deal."

"Is that why you're so ambitious?"

"Yes, funny isn't it? It's great to have money to do things with, but sometimes I think I'm tired of the corporate world already. It was nice of you to come with us to dinner last night. I needed someone to be there. And the walk along the canal was super. I want my boyfriend to meet Dad, but I know it won't go well. Dad tells me you've been through a lot, too."

"Not so much," Gigi said.

"Dad told me last night that when you leave Japan, he needs to go to the mountain where Curt disappeared. When it happened, he'd thought he might move to the village at the foot of the mountain to be near my brother.

Gigi couldn't see the man Amanda said Richard was even now. Sometimes distrustful, cold, angry.

"And anyways," Amanda said, "he always liked my brother better. I think he really loved him."

Gigi wanted to say, I know he loves you, but she didn't. She had no idea if it was the truth. Instead, she put her hand on Amanda's shoulder. Soon Richard might open the door to his apartment and see them sitting on the couch together. She wasn't sure he'd like that. He'd never invited her into his place.

"At least he seemed really happy to see me. At least I listened to him without storming out of the apartment. At least we sat at the table and ate together. We looked out at the canal and the lights and the sky. It was great. We'd hardly said anything to each other for such a long time."

The noise from the trucks going over the bridge above the river stopped for a minute. Or maybe it was her heart that stopped beating. Why had she left her sons? She was so far away and the thought of them made her close her eyes so she could imagine she was home. She thought about the years with her husband. How, when they were all together, she felt like her husband and sons had a club that she was not quite a member of, yet they were woven into her heart.

EIGHTY-TWO

Gigi took the elevator down from the eleventh floor. She was trying not to cry on the way down. She walked quickly across the small lobby. The building door slid open. She walked around the corner to the wooden ramp leading to the walkway along the canal. She wasn't sure what she'd do. It was already unbearably hot, even though she was used to it. She wiped her eyes and sat down on the bench below her balcony where the blackbirds squabbled and the women weeded the garden wearing their big hats.

Was Richard's past something he couldn't talk about, really? He'd kept her out of the most intimate parts of his life. He must be upset about the way his daughter felt about him. His son's tragic death. She wouldn't know what to do if she lost one of her sons. But didn't she also have a right to be bitter about losing so much of herself? She knew these feelings didn't go away. They just simmered underneath.

She was sticky. Her cotton pants were wet. Her head ached. The silent heron flying above her, the rumble of the monorail. The dark water of the canal sloshing against the concrete bank. The ferry that never arrived, the bus going past her at one stop first and then another. The children running behind a fence, kicking a soccer ball this way and that on the green lawn. The tightly wrapped buildings under construction.

Soon, though, the 100-year-old man was coming toward her, his white wide brimmed hat pulled down across his brow. He wore a seersucker suit and a white shirt open at the throat. He carried a slim briefcase. Gigi wasn't sure he could see her as he sat down on the bench.

"I once wished I could live forever, and now I have. You're still young," he said looking at Gigi from under his hat.

Gigi laughed.

"I was very rich, and I didn't have to work, though my father sent me out to rice fields when I was a little boy so I could understand what it was like to bend over the shining water. When I was thirty, I'd seen quite a lot living in the city. That was when the firebombs came and everything, it seemed, was up in flames. This canal, the little house where I went to have sake, the place where the geishas massaged my feet, the jewelry store where I bought emeralds for the women I loved."

"It must have been awful," Gigi said.

"Yes, but I had friends who were poets and we met in a hut on a lake and drank to the moon. Even after the fires, I had a great desire to live for almost 500 years. I knew there was a princess in Yamato who lived that long, and when she died the kingdom built a tomb for her on an island. You can go there still and see the trees that circle the sacred place, but don't try to walk up to the tomb itself. They'll shoot you.

"I heard about a Chinese emperor who lived a very long life because he'd found the elixir of life. He'd traveled to some place far away where there were hermits who lived at the top of the sacred mountain shaped like a white cone. It sounded very much like Fuji. And here I was on the island where the magic mountain was. I climbed to the top of the mountain and there were no hermits there, just monks trying to sell me things."

"Did you ever find the elixir?" Gigi asked.

"No," he said, "but I prayed to Jofuko, who said to me, You, Sentaro, are fond of living and every comfort. Your desire is a very selfish one and cannot be easily granted. Do you know how hard a hermit's life is? A hermit is only allowed to eat fruit and berries and the bark of pine trees. A hermit must cut himself off from the world so his heart is as pure as gold and free from all earthly desires. Gradually, after following these strict rules, the hermit ceases to feel hunger or cold or heat, and his body becomes so light that he can ride on a crane or a carp and can walk on water without getting his feet wet.

"He gave me this little crane," Sentaro said and put his hand in the pocket of his jacket. On his palm was a paper crane. "I won't tell you what happened next because you won't believe me."

Gigi looked up. Richard was walking toward them on the path from the direction of the bay. You could imagine the ocean there, though there were buildings and overpasses blocking the way to the water.

"But here I am. I could be 500 years old if I wanted to live that long but I don't. I think because I didn't really keep the bargain, I'll only make it to a little over 100 and that's fine with me. How can a body carry a soul for much more than that? I think in the end Jofuko sent me a dream of the place where there's eternal life, and that was enough to make me happy to be here. There were so many bored old people. Picking their nails and looking off at the sea."

Richard had been walking very fast and he slowed down when he saw her.

The ancient man laughed and put his hand on Gigi's arm and nodded toward Richard. He pushed himself up from the bench as Richard walked toward her. Below them in the canal a family of ordinary ducks swam toward the bay.

Why didn't you tell me about your son," she said, when he was a few feet away.

"I don't want to do this."

"What?" She stood up and faced him.

"Have this conversation."

A woman passed them carrying a tiny baby in a snuggly.

"You lied to me. You made me think your son was just far away in some wild place," Gigi said.

"I can't talk about it."

"I thought we were close."

"We are."

"No, we aren't, if you can't tell me about his death. There's nothing between us, really."

"I wasn't sure there was."

"You keep pulling away," she said and looked out at the water.

"Only because you seem so uneasy."

"Not all the time."

"No, but it's an impossible situation. I can tell you've decided it's not worth it after all you've been through."

"How do you know that?"

"Because of how you're acting now. You're never angry. Obstinate but not mad."

"Are you?" she asked.

"Yes, often. But I usually spend a lot of time alone."

And then he did something he'd never done before. He reached out and pulled her closer and put his arms around her. She closed her eyes and took a deep breath. It was a moment that didn't last very long, but she knew it was something she'd desperately wanted. To feel his arms around her.

"I'm so sorry about your son," she said against his shoulder.

"You know, when I first met you I thought you were magical. It was a surprise, wanting something all of a sudden like this. It made me feel out of control, haphazard. I didn't want to feel anything for anyone. What I felt for you was perplexing. It made me uneasy. I wanted to be stripped of all emotions. It was just too much. I wanted my body to be the only emotion I felt—the movement of my body dipping and swirling."

His chin was against her hair. She could feel the warmth from his breath.

"When my son was lost, time was porous. Doing zazen did nothing to erase the pain. It wasn't a nightmare, just something I couldn't do anything about then, even though I'd mastered other ways of thinking that were much more difficult. He was always getting himself into some kind of trouble. Curt was impulsive and very smart. I rocked him for hours when he was a baby. I can still feel his soft hair against my cheek."

EIGHTY-THREE

She was walking home from her last Ikebana class, her bundle of cut flowers wrapped in the pink plastic carrier. The bending green fronds of a tropical plant, yellow lilies budded but not blooming, and the third flower, the straight furry nubs of the purple liatris. She felt like she knew these flowers better than she'd known most of the plants in her life. She watched her teacher bend and twist the green fronds into curves and anchor the arrangement with the lilies and give the whole composition energy with the purple spikes of the liatris.

Now all she had to do was reproduce her arrangement at home on the coffee table in a plastic tray she'd gotten from the 100-yen store where she bought bags of soil and pots and pink gloves and wire and pans and cups and glasses.

The owner had giggled when she appeared at the counter again and again with one more thing. Her latest purchases were red plaid slippers to bring home and a special Japanese saw for her husband. A Shark two-handed pull saw. Soon she'd fly home over the shimmering fields ripe now with rice.

As she walked up the hill she adjusted the bundle in her arms. The cemetery was on her left, after she passed the shed with two benches filled with bonsai. She looked down at the hundreds of *sotoba* on the graves. Kanji incised on the narrow wooden planks with sacred wishes for the dead.

The street was steep and once at the top of the hill, she was near the courtyards of comfortable upscale houses. Trimmed bushes and tall trees arched over the concrete walls of the homes. Children were playing hockey in a field behind a fence. A guard in a dark blue uniform and a braided cap stood at attention near the gate. All along the wall bordering the right side sunflowers were blooming. Their bright faces followed her.

Her teacher had adjusted one of the spikes of liatris in Gigi's arrangement at the end of the class. "Now the line is stronger," she said. "But the whole is very fine."

"Sensei," one of the women said, "can you stand by your flowers and I'll take your picture?"

They'd displayed their arrangements one by one and Risen had snapped pictures of the flowers against the white wall. Gigi was hoping she'd understood each flower's essence and her teacher would be pleased.

The handout Risen gave the class explained that the three lines were part of the new style or *seika* in Tokyo in the eighteenth century. They expressed the universe of Confucianism. *Ten*, sky or nature; *chi*, ground; and *jin*, man. Her teacher told them practicing the art of Ikebana gives a sense of peace and serenity.

When she got home, she spent quite a long time arranging the flowers again. There was a slight breeze and she sat out on the balcony on her folding chair until the trucks stopped clattering across the bridge. For a moment everything was still.

EIGHTY-FOUR

Motoko had finally talked her into going to an *onsen*. The most beautiful one near Tokyo. A whole village full of ancient *ryokan* inland from the coast where they'd walked on the cliffs above the turquoise water.

"We might even go scuba diving on the way home," she said. "Remember we saw that guy and his students? Near the little beach?"

"Yes."

A driver met them at the train and they loaded their small bags into the trunk. He snapped the lid closed and adjusted his white gloves.

They rushed by pine trees clinging to the cliffs along the ocean.

The perfectly clear water shimmered. Dotting the coast were little rocks with their own trees holding onto the surface as waves broke around the islands. Gigi was perfectly happy to be sitting in the speeding cab next to Motoko on her way to the *onsen*. They turned inland and came to the village along the rocky river. The wooden inns leaned over the water.

Their *ryokan* was in a bamboo grove. Each room had a little porch and its own garden.

"The mineral content of the water is great here. Very healing," Motoko said. They'd brought towels, one large and one small from their room. The outdoor pool was surrounded by rocks. The river meandered below them, the water low this time of year. Soon, Motoko told her, the trees would be blazing with red leaves all up and down the riverbank.

They walked slowly from their room to the women's bath, red curtains hanging from the top of the doorway. There was a row of showers like in a changing room at a public pool. They took off their clothes and folded them carefully on a bench. Motoko had told her she should rinse off and then sit on the wooden stool, the bamboo bucket at her feet, and wash herself with the little cloth and then rinse again. The same little cloth that she'd use to cover herself as she walked to the hot pool. How could she hide anything with a towel the size of a washcloth?

She always felt uneasy taking her clothes off in front of strangers. Especially in changing rooms. She held her tiny towel in front of her trying to cover everything until she was near the pool. It was a relief to get it over with and immerse herself in the bubbling water.

The waves sloshed around her shoulders as one and then another woman joined them. They had already washed and lathered and rinsed. She liked the idea of cleansing your body and then joining your neighbors in the bath, even if the ritual made her uncomfortable.

The women moved around her in the water, laughing and talking. To commiserate, exchange stories. Talk about your children, Motoko had told her.

"Don't put the towel in the water," Motoko said. "You can set it on the side of the pool and rest your head if you want."

Before she went to the *onsen* she'd clipped her toenails. It was such an easy thing to do, but it had taken her months after her stroke before she could lift her leg up on her lap and grasp her toes to clip each nail. Her physical therapist, Bill, had her practice each movement until her body understood what she had to do. It was the same with rolling up off the floor, such an easy thing to do before the lightning struck. Her left side was weaker than the right and that was par for the course they told her. But she would get stronger, Bill said, just wait.

It was perfectly possible even in this world. They had to keep putting in requests for more therapy and Bill had to sign off on the request. She was improving, she was continuing to improve, this was not a waste of the insurance company's money. She pedaled on the stationary bike for at first one minute and then five and then ten. As her husband walked beside her in the halls, she pushed herself to step up the pace and move both her arms, not just one.

She knew there wasn't any way to figure out what was fate and what was not. It wasn't fate, was it, to have met Richard here in the ancient country where persimmons were wrapped in leaves on their branches or trees were hidden in the hollows of the very old garden behind the baseball stadium? It wasn't fate to feel something again after all those months and years of fighting to have her brain back. Her emotions checked at the door after the rehab made her new again. She wanted to think there was an order to the universe. The tall trees that looked artificial above the tracks so close together that you couldn't fit a hand between them, the threading needle of the station where all the trains met and then took off. A kind of design. But whenever she thought, ah, that's why that happened, it wasn't at all why something happened. Her miscarriage wasn't the price for her two sons. She'd lost the first child to have first one and then another.

And what about the loss she felt now? Richard had gone to the village near where his son had died. He hadn't waited until she was back in Tokyo to say goodbye.

Motoko was leaning against the stone lip of the pool, her head on the small white towel. Her dark hair streaked with pink was pulled up in a twist on the top of her head. Gigi placed her towel on the edge.

"Don't swim whatever you do," Motoko said. "Just relax."

Gigi hadn't been in a public sauna for years and that was when she was slim and young and her skin was firm. It didn't seem to make any difference here. Many of the women were older than she was and they stepped carefully into the pool.

Motoko smiled. "Wonderful, isn't it? See, you had nothing to worry about."

The water was bubbling and warm. It smelled like the mountains, she thought. That clean metallic smell of stones and pine.

Motoko leaned closer to Gigi. "What happened on your trip to Tohoku with Richard?"

"I suppose it was both funny and tragic. His friend's house was abandoned. It was my fault we were almost killed by two yakuza who had potbellies and gray hair."

"Oh my god," she said, "what did you do to make them angry?"

"We let their wild boar go. A whole family."

"No!"

"Yes. They tied us up with zip ties and drove off. I was freaked out."

"And you escaped?"

"Yup."

The water was making Gigi sleepy. "I'm both sad and happy," she said, "to be going home. Richard and I had an argument and I won't see him again now before I leave. His son Curt died years ago and he didn't tell me. He has a little altar in his apartment with a small statue of the Buddha. There's a picture of his son on the top of Mount Fuji beside the Buddha."

"That's got to be so tragic."

"Yes. He told me so many things, but not the most important."

"Sometimes that's impossible if you want to hold yourself together." She dipped under the water and popped up again.

"So you love your husband more than you thought?" Motoko laughed.

"I don't think I thought about it very much. I just accepted it. Like air. And now I can't wait to see him."

"I loved a sculptor once a few years ago. My mother had told me when I was younger it was a bad idea to love an artist. She'd experienced that with my father. Their work will always be more important than you. But she was funny and had beautiful eyes and laughed a lot."

"What happened?"

"She moved back to Osaka. She had a life there. I wanted to stay in Tokyo. It didn't seem like I loved her enough to follow her."

Gigi thought about Richard's arms around her, his lips against her hair, the sour smell of the water, a gull squawking, flying above the 100-year-old man who watched them from the path.

EIGHTY-FIVE

They were about two hours up the trail on the holy mountain when the monk, or priest, appeared. She wasn't sure what he was called. A pelt attached to his belt covered his hips like a fat tail. He was dressed in billowing white pants and a white shirt. There were no stains on his clothes. He wore a white cloth headband around his forehead. A little black round box was stitched to the front of the headband.

He leaned on his long pole as he climbed up the slope of crumbling rocks. On the top of the pole was a metal ornament. He'd belted his pants with an orange climbing rope. A bell attached to his belt chimed when he walked. He seemed to be counting.

Gigi had been concentrating on the flowers. They were like flowers in Dutch paintings of the golden age. Delicate and many flowered orange lilies. Motoko handed her a bag of apricots and she took two.

SHARON WHITE

She put one of the fruits into her mouth and chewed slowly.

The monk passed them, huffing as he pulled himself up the steep trail.

She was feeling quite fit, she thought. Her thigh muscles tingled with the climb, not at all like when she went up the sacred mountain with the kids from her class. Not at all.

Something had happened to her over the months she'd been in the ancient country. And it had nothing to do with what she felt for Richard.

Motoko was standing on the edge of the trail now, her back to her, looking into the deep woods. There was bamboo on the edge of the woods and beyond that the puffy cedars called cryptomeria. They were unlike anything you saw at home. Everything was different and her skin had absorbed the smell of the newness.

"Ready?" she asked and smiled as Motoko turned. Gigi pulled on her pack and adjusted the belt. They carried extra clothes, hiking umbrellas, raincoats and pants. You never could tell what was going to happen in the mountains.

"Was he a priest?"

"*Shugenja*," Motoko said. "A Shinto priest."

"With a backpack and hiking boots?" she laughed.

"Why not? He may have been walking for days."

SHARON WHITE

ACKNOWLEDGEMENTS

A big hug to Felicity Blundon, Karen Donovan, Sharon Kirsch, and Elaine Terranova, my cheerleaders, for their attentive comments on this book. I'm grateful to friend and garden historian Mark Laird for pointing the way to discussions of Japanese gardens. Thank you to Kristina Marie Darling, Karen Joy Fowler, Ann Hood, and Sherri Smith for their generous encouragement.

Special thanks to Kim Brown, publisher and executive editor, Minerva Rising Press, for her thoughtful editing.

Some of the chapters in Minato Sketches have appeared in Tupelo Quarterly and Philadelphia Stories.

Many thanks to the Caselberg Trust, Broad Bay, New Zealand and the Creator-in-Residence program, Hillswick, Shetland for residencies.

Books I found helpful are *Irradiated Cities*, Mariko Nagai;

Horses, Horses, in the End the Light Remains Pure: A Tale That Begins With Fukushima, Hideo Furukawa, translated by Doug Slaymaker with Akiko Takenaka; *Surviving the 2011 Tsunami: 100 Testimonies of Ishinomaki Area Survivors of the Great East Japan Earthquake,* Editorial Office of the Ishinomaki Kahoku; *Lost Japan, Last Glimpse of Beautiful Japan,* Alex Kerr; and *Sacred Cesium Ground and Isa's Deluge,* Kimura Yusuke, translated by Doug Slaymaker.

The tale in Chapter 82 is a variation on "The Story of the Man Who Did Not Wish to Die" in *Japanese Fairy Tales,* compiled by Yei Theodora Ozaki.

Scott and Graham continue to entertain me through thick and thin.

ABOUT THE AUTHOR

Sharon White is the author of several books of nonfiction, poetry, and fiction, including *Vanished Gardens: Finding Nature in Philadelphia,* winner of the AWP award in creative nonfiction. Her latest collection of poetry is *The Body is Burden and Delight. Boiling Lake (On Voyage)* won the Italo Calvino Prize in Fabulist Fiction. *Field Notes, A Geography of Mourning,* received the Julia Ward Howe Prize, Honorable Mention, from the Boston Authors Club. Some of her other awards include the Marguerite McGlinn Prize for Fiction from *Philadelphia Stories* for *Minato Sketches*, the Neil Shepard Prize, *Green Mountains Review,* a Pennsylvania Council on the Arts Fellowship, the Leeway Foundation Award for Achievement, a Colorado Council on the Arts Fellowship, and a National Endowment for the Arts Fellowship. She is an Associate Professor Emerita at Temple University.